She needed his touch— needed it desperately

"Look at me, Caburn," Anna begged. "Don't you think I can please you? Don't you think I'm beautiful?"

Caburn swallowed. There was no turning away from her now—not when she needed him like this. He could feel himself losing control and couldn't keep from touching her. When he crushed her to him she smelled of rain and tears and flowers.

Anna didn't think about what was happening. "Tell me I'm beautiful Caburn," she implored. "Tell me I'm loved—make me believe!"

"You're going to regret this, my darling," he answered hoarsely. "But you *are* beautiful, and I want you so much. . . ."

THE AUTHOR

Jackie Weger's home is in Fort Bend County, Texas, but she has traveled widely in her lifetime. She does on-site research for every book she writes; *Winter Song* reflects moods and details of the week she spent exploring Washington, D.C.

Jackie's now working on her next Temptation, set in the fascinating bayou country of Louisiana. Predictably, she insisted on doing firsthand research into the fur-trapping industry there—in early spring. She came home with a wealth of information and a bad cold.

Books by Jackie Weger

HARLEQUIN TEMPTATIONS
 7—CAST A GOLDEN SHADOW
29—WINTER SONG

HARLEQUIN AMERICAN ROMANCES
 5—A STRONG AND TENDER THREAD
48—COUNT THE ROSES

These books may be available at your local bookseller.

Don't miss any of our special offers. Write to us at the following address for information on our newest releases.

Harlequin Reader Service
P.O. Box 52040, Phoenix, AZ 85072-2040
Canadian address: P.O. Box 2800, Postal Station A,
5170 Yonge St., Willowdale, Ont. M2N 5T5

Winter Song

JACKIE WEGER

Harlequin Books

TORONTO • NEW YORK • LONDON
AMSTERDAM • PARIS • SYDNEY • HAMBURG
STOCKHOLM • ATHENS • TOKYO • MILAN

Published October 1984

ISBN 0-373-25129-7

Printed in Canada

1

As Anna Nesmith tugged on a white velour caftan, its cool silk lining whispered over her supple flesh, making her nipples come erect. For an instant she stood very still, trying to disengage her mind from her body's reaction to the silk, but the mental trick didn't work. "Kevin...Kevin..." she pleaded silently. "You've got to find time for me—and soon."

She suppressed a sigh. There was no point in thinking about it, but lately there always seemed to be some reason they couldn't make love: Kevin was called in to work on his days off, just when she had planned a cozy interlude, or he was so tired—she joked about that. Jet lag, he said. Or his mother, Clara Alice, wasn't feeling well and bedroom doors had to be left open.

Sometimes Anna could feel the longing building up until she didn't know how she could bear it. She tried to be understanding, yet everything her eye touched these days seemed to have some sort of sensual symbolism, like the Renoir print, *Le bal a Bourgival*, hanging nearby on the textured gray wall. The couple portrayed actually seemed to be moving in their dancing embrace, and in her mind Anna carried their delicately painted movements into bed. Over by the window was the chaise longue, covered in pink satin—an ordinary piece of furniture—yet she saw herself lying upon it naked, beckoning to Kevin. The picture stayed with her until a tiny moan burst from her throat.

Parts of her were clamoring for attention, parts she tried to ignore, parts she tried to pretend didn't exist anymore. Driven by her thoughts, Anna went to her husband's closet and opened the door. The man smell of him lingered in his clothes, in his suits, in his wool sweaters. She took one of his sweaters and buried her face in its soft fleece, wondering how a man in the prime of his life could exert such control over his emotions. She couldn't help wondering what was so wrong with her, so wrong with their marriage that her husband wanted her so seldom.

Angry at herself for letting her thoughts take the turn they had, Anna did a mental inventory. She had Kevin's approval, she was certain of that. She could cook; she kept the house clean, elegant even—when Clara Alice wasn't changing the furniture around. Too, she had a well-paying job, though not exciting, working in Senate Research Services at the Library of Congress, and that brought in needed cash.

On the physical side she wasn't pencil thin, but all soft curves and her flesh seemed to hug her bones. She wore her richly brown hair parted in the middle, so that it framed her face and loosely brushed her shoulders. There was even more brown in her eyes. A friend had once said that Anna had eyes that lived, that saw and recorded life, but all she saw these past weeks were eyes that hid her unrest. She had one of those oval faces people always thought were so photogenic, but in her case truly had no planes to shadow, no compression, no sultriness; and yet it was a face having its own character in the high forehead and the lovely shaped mouth. The funny part, Anna thought, was that she didn't photograph well at all.

Without knocking, Clara Alice came bursting into her bedroom, startling Anna from her reverie. She dropped the sweater and hurried to her mother-in-law's side. Always high-strung, Clara Alice's entire stocky body was now shaking. Alarmed, Anna grabbed her by the arm, dragging her over to the chaise longue.

"You're as white as a sheet, Clara Alice. What's wrong? Are you having another attack?"

"There's a strange man at the door!"

Anna let her hands fall to her sides, her fear for Clara Alice subsiding. She should've known. This was another of her mother-in-law's false alarms, but still, her nervous excitement had to be calmed. "It's probably just a neighbor, nothing to get upset about."

"But I know all the neighbors now, don't I? It's the same man who parked right behind you when you came home. I told you, but you didn't listen. You never listen to me. He's followed you, that's what!"

Anna's hand moved in a tiny unnoticed gesture of resignation. "I'll go see who it is."

Anna, Kevin and his mother lived in one of the older neighborhoods in Washington that wasn't backed up to a ghetto, a government building or an exquisite brownstone. In the two years they had lived there, Anna had noticed subtle signs of deterioration along the old boulevard, but nothing so alarming that Clara Alice should fear opening the door.

Anna wasn't especially concerned now as she left her mother-in-law's side. But she couldn't bear another lecture from Kevin about his mother. She couldn't bear the way his lips tightened when Clara Alice complained about how she was treated. If Kevin was home more, he would see for himself how impossible their situation was becoming.

Anna heard the knocking as she emerged into the hall. It had the insistent tattoo of a hammer being

wielded by an angry man. She was sensitive to
sounds, preferring them soft, musical. Part of her
was furious with Clara Alice, and another with this
man who had the gall to pound so irreverently on
her door.

She put her eye to the viewer.

Though the porch light was faint, she could still
make out details. He looked to be a man who had
done everything once—twice, if he liked it. He had
one of those rugged complexions that sit well on
blond men, every line put there by some triumphant
conquest. There was an old scar on the side of his
nose that lost itself in a thick mustache, precisely
clipped so that it didn't hide a firm upper lip. His
crisp blond hair, given to curl, was trimmed military
short around his ears, and he wore a gray overcoat
that gave substance to broad shoulders. He wasn't
overly tall, perhaps five feet ten or eleven inches,
and carried himself with a warrior's insolence. His
eyes were some dark color, and even through the
narrow aperture Anna could see them flashing with
impatience. She saw his fist come up to knock again.

"Who are you? What do you want?" She spoke
quickly.

"Government business, Mrs. Nesmith. May I come
in?"

It was a strong clear voice, armed with authority.
Anna was suddenly filled with a cold sickening
dread. Something must have happened to Kevin.
Fear made her heart race, sent blood pounding in
her head. She was only partly aware of Clara Alice
hovering nervously behind her.

"Don't let him in no matter what," urged the old
woman. "It's a trick. We'll be raped."

"Be quiet a minute, Clara Alice...please," Anna
hissed. To the man on the opposite side of the door
she said with caution, "What kind of business? Put

your identification where I can see it." She wanted desperately to fling open the door to ask about Kevin, but was afraid of the answer she might get.

An official badge encased in a wallet flashed before her. It showed a photograph and ID, which she couldn't read clearly in the dim yellow light. "Open up, Mrs. Nesmith," he said again, exasperation overlaying the tone of authority. "I'm from State. We're doing routine security checks on our couriers. Also, it's as cold as hell out here."

"Routine," Anna breathed, relief making her feel weak. There was nothing wrong. She waved Clara Alice back and opened the door slowly. Wind and snow swirled past her. She half expected the man to push his way across the threshold. He didn't, but held his position on the porch, allowing her time for a closer inspection.

Anna's hand fluttered to her throat in a protective reflex. Before her stood a man with an aura of power, and she felt it envelop her physically, like a mist rolling off a river. It struck her sensibilities so strongly that she continued to stand there and gape.

A part of her knew her feet were firmly planted on the small Rumanian kilim rug she had bought from a departing senator's wife, yet she had a curious feeling of being suspended in space; a human island anchored to nothing beyond a wisp of cloud. She didn't need intuition to warn her that he was dangerous. The man exuded a mixture of power and menace and agitation. It sent a current up her spine.

"Have you ever killed anybody?" she blurted.

Francis Caburn was aware of the effect he had on people, especially women, but not one had ever greeted him with so astonishing a question. He knew he was skillful as an interrogator, shrewd, well informed, tough-minded and tenacious. And that when the occasion demanded, he could be exceedingly charming. This might, he mused, be one of those times.

Though he had been in battles, survived them and looked it, not visible was an eccentricity he suffered that bordered on the phobic. He was scared of heights. He refused to ride in elevators that zipped up the sides of buildings, to climb ladders or to eat in rooftop restaurants with a view. He couldn't credit it, but right now, gazing into the striking questioning face of Anna Nesmith, he had the same dizzying sensation he'd had the first time his stepfather had sent him atop the grain silo to check the level of wheat stored there.

He became aware that snow was flying around him, catching on his eyelashes. He blinked, realizing she was still waiting for an answer. He made a mental adjustment. In his work he was used to fabricating stories on the periphery of truth, but some deeper dimension made him speak now with a candor he seldom revealed.

"In war," he said, "when it was me or them."

"You can't come in my house," she said, beginning to close the door and retreating behind it.

His foot shot out. It was the first time the initiative had been so smoothly snatched from him by a woman. "Hold it, Mrs. Nesmith, I have to talk to you. I'm from the Department of—"

"I heard you the first time." She was suffering as much from a reluctant curiosity as from the bitter cold sweeping into the foyer.

Sensing her willingness to listen, Caburn changed tactics. "I just need you to answer a few simple questions. If it's a bother now, perhaps you could come down to my office in the morning...?"

"I can't. I have to work."

He shrugged. "Whichever is more convenient. Your husband is Kevin Nesmith, courier for—"

"Yes." Anna bit her lip, hesitating a few seconds more. Though the man gave the impression of being tough, he somehow had managed to preserve a certain basic vulnerability. There was just a hint of it in his stance. She stepped back into the foyer. "I guess you can come in."

As he followed her, angling around an oddly placed table, Caburn caught sight of a grim-faced old woman. He nodded in a wordless unsmiling greeting.

"My mother-in-law," Anna murmured as she took refuge in the wing chair she most often sat in, curling her feet beneath her. The strange effect the man was having upon her coupled with the unusual placement of the furniture, thanks to Clara Alice, left Anna uncomfortable in her familiar surroundings. And she was aware, too, that under the caftan she was wholly naked.

Caburn sat on the sofa, his antennae keen. Lurking beneath the perfume Anna wore was a woman scent, inexorably sensual, not the sort of thing one noticed from across a room, but he was in her space now, studying her posture, her face. There was a fragile quality about her...trusting; he was seized with a feeling of protectiveness toward her. "Why did you ask if I had killed anyone?" he asked.

"You look like you have," she answered in a small voice because her breath was lodging in her throat. The intensity of his gaze was making her nervous and she let her gaze slide away.

"I didn't mean to frighten you."

"I was just surprised, that's all." Her tentative smile was laced with a trace of anxiety as she made an effort at being cordial. "What was your name again?"

Clara Alice chose that moment to become aggressive, thrusting herself into the crowded space between Anna and the investigator, parking her hands on wide hips in a stance Anna knew well. "Just who are you?" she demanded. "What do you want with my son? Security check, indeed! Kevin is as honest as the day is long. You ought to be out looking for real criminals. Well, speak up," she huffed, double chins quaking.

Mortified, Anna wanted to bury her face in her hands. Regardless of why the man was here, Kevin's job could be on the line. Some situations called for a delicacy that was beyond Clara Alice, but she just never seemed to know when to keep quiet. A person more observant than her mother-in-law might have noticed the tightening of their visitor's jaw, the hardness of his gaze, and been warned. But Clara Alice was not one to take heed.

"My name's Caburn." His tone of harsh authority was back. "I'll be here a few minutes on government business." He paused to let that sink in, his tone stating what his words had not—he wouldn't tolerate interference under any circumstances. His next comment was an order, with none of the deference Clara Alice demanded as her due. "Why don't you bring us coffee?"

Anna watched, breathless, as in a calculated flurry of busyness he brushed snow from his blond hair, hiked up his tweed slacks at the knees and crossed his legs. Clara Alice had been dismissed and knew it. Had the circumstances been different, Anna might have warmed to her uninvited guest, but he had a disquieting presence that filled the room. She could sense that he knew it, that he knew it was affecting her. He didn't raise his eyes to hers until Clara Alice had retreated from the room. Then she saw that they were slate gray—flat, cold and ruthless.

She clasped her hands tightly in her lap.

"Terrible storm," he said finally. "For a change, it's got everybody railing at the weather or God, instead of the president."

"You can leave off the small talk," she replied, feeling tenser because she knew he was trying to put her at ease. "What's your title again? Lieutenant? Captain? Major?" His gray eyes flickered with impatience.

"Just Caburn, Mrs. Nesmith. I'm a civilian employee just like your husband."

"Not quite like my husband," she said. Kevin's military background hadn't left him with an arrogant, power-filled aura that seemed to be second nature to this man. "If you aren't military now, you have been," she stated firmly. "May I see your identification again, please?" It was a request she knew he couldn't refuse.

He whipped the ID out as if it was carrion picked over by vultures. Anna leaned forward, took the card and perused it. "Oh," she said. "*Francis* Caburn." She passed the ID back to him.

"Just Caburn," he reiterated, his tone the same as he had used on Clara Alice as his eyes narrowed and locked on her.

He had no right to take that tone with her. "Of course," she said perversely. "No one calls you Francis but your mother."

"That's right—no one but my mother." He spoke so softly Anna could tell she had touched a raw buried nerve. It gave her an odd sense of pleasure to know that she had inadvertently penetrated his steellike exterior, perhaps had touched on the vulnerability she had sensed earlier.

"Now, if you don't mind," he ventured in a tone that said he didn't give a damn whether she did or not, "I'd like to get this over with. It's getting late."

Anna's chin went up. "Certainly I don't mind. I

wish you would. You've interrupted our dinner. We've never had a security check at the house before. What's brought this one on?" Caburn's mouth drew into a thin hard line below the precisely clipped mustache. Anna could almost see his brain flexing. A slight feeling of renewed alarm assailed her. He wasn't going to give her a reply. "Is my husband all right?"

"Why shouldn't he be?" came the swift retort, putting Anna off the small measure of balance she had managed to retain.

"Well...the nature of his work...."

"The nature of his work..." Caburn murmured, as if he'd only just thought of it. "Does he talk about it?"

No, Anna thought, *he doesn't talk about it. He hardly talks at all these days. Not to me or his mother. He doesn't do a lot of things we used to do. Sometimes he sits and stares at me, and when I find him doing it, he turns away as if he can't abide looking at me.* She was coming dangerously close to a subject she didn't want to face, and a trace of irritation rose within her that a stranger had provoked unsettling thoughts. "Look, Caburn, or mercenary, or investigator, or whatever you call yourself, my husband is a diplomatic courier. He carries sensitive documents. I know it, he knows it. If you're asking does he talk in his sleep, the answer is no. We don't discuss what he carries, and only occasionally where he delivers it."

He used to bring her little nonsensical gifts, she remembered...paper flowers, a funny little card written in French or Japanese or a perfume sample from one of the designer houses. But he didn't do that anymore, either.

"I see," said Caburn, acting as though he didn't and trying to decide if now was the best time to deflate her anger. Angry people tended to say more than calm ones. He needed more facts. Too, he had an uneasy feeling her anger wasn't wholly directed toward himself.

Bearing a tray with coffee and only two cups and saucers, Clara Alice bustled into the room. She placed the tray none too gently on the oak table between Anna and Caburn. "You can pour, Anna. I'll be in my room watching television...with the door open, if you need me." Caburn might not have existed.

"Thank you," Anna murmured. She unfolded her legs, leaning forward, and Caburn got a glimpse of softly rounded pink flesh as the décolletage of her caftan gaped. Anna lifted her eyes as she passed him coffee and discerned the reason for his stare. A warm flush rose up the slender column of her neck to flare in her cheeks. In that instant she recognized that Francis Caburn represented not only risk to Kevin, but a more ancient, more common, easily named risk to herself. It wasn't a revelation she liked knowing about herself. Or him.

"Your coffee," she said stiffly. The cup tottered in its saucer, betraying her anxiety.

He took several tentative sips. "Good coffee," he said, giving her a slow intimate smile.

He looked different when his lips curved upward. She felt herself being pulled into his aura, acknowledging that she was drawn to him in a very sexual way. She smiled faintly back at him over the rim of her cup, fearing that there was about her some invisible clue that marked her longing.

"How long have you lived in Washington?" he asked with deceptive sociability.

"Two years."

"Like what you find here?"

She gave a small laugh. "I loved the weather, until this week. I keep telling myself that I'm going to do the grand tour, but living just seems to keep getting in the way.''

Truth was, Kevin had rebelled at sight-seeing, and Clara Alice, in the year she'd been with them, insisted she was not yet well enough to do all that much walking.

He gave her another of his half smiles. She followed the curve of his mouth to his eyes and was startled to find that the smile did not go beyond his lips. A chill coursed up her spine.

"How many bank accounts do you have, Mrs. Nesmith?"

"I . . . beg your pardon?"

"No need for that. Just answer my question." There was a cutting edge to his voice. Anna felt she had been duped, softened up for the kill.

"I don't handle the finances. My husband takes care of all that."

One blond eyebrow rose in skepticism. "You don't know anything about how and where the money goes in this household?"

"Of course I know. I just don't write out the checks or make the deposits." He was hearing every word she said, but his eyes now were darting around the room, recording, Anna thought, taking in quality and quantity. She put her cup and saucer down on the table with a sharp clatter. "Please leave, Mr. Caburn. Take this up with my husband when he comes home."

His lids dropped perceptibly. "In a moment, please. I only have another question or two."

"Well, ask them and get out," she reiterated, looking past him, staring at nothing, feeling more feminine in his presence than she had in months and then reproaching herself for it because the wrong man, an absolute stranger, had caused the feeling to sweep over her.

Caburn picked up the scarab paperweight from the small table at his elbow, examining it, feeling the cool bonded bronze begin to warm in his hand. "Were you aware Nesmith handled dispatches during the SALT conferences?"

"How could I not be?" She knew her lips shaped the words, made sounds, but they had a far-off quality, like a dream. She still wasn't looking at Caburn. "I was delighted that the talks collapsed. Kevin managed an entire day home."

That was the day she had broached the topic of having a baby. Kevin had said it was too costly, that they couldn't afford for her to quit work yet; but he hadn't said no. And she had quietly and secretly stopped using any prevention. She was thirty-two, and she wanted to experience pregnancy. It was an old instinctive urge, but nothing had happened so far, and the fear was growing that she couldn't have a baby.

Caburn saw the tiny smile at the corner of Anna's mouth, saw the warm glow in her eyes as she thought of her husband. He felt a surge of anger begin to burn deep within himself. *Some women have lousy luck*, he thought, and suddenly stood up. "I'll be going now, Mrs. Nesmith. We'll continue this later."

His lithe unexpected movement yanked Anna back to the present. "Continue? But why? You see how we live, Kevin's life—our life—is an open book. He goes to work and comes home. Talk to him when he gets back. Surely—"

An open book with a few secret pages, Caburn was thinking. "Where were you born, Mrs. Nesmith?"

"Kansas City, Kansas. You're confusing me. I don't need a clearance. I'm a librarian."

He ignored her protests. "When were you born?"

"In October. This month. I just had a birthday." And Kevin forgot it, she remembered, frowning.

"October...that makes you a Libra, doesn't it? The kind of woman who lures a man without yielding to his carnal passions...?" He let the sentence hang in the air between them.

Anna rose to her feet, summoning an immense dignity she never once suspected she owned. "Do you mean to tell me the federal government is hiring fortune-tellers and astrologers for investigators these days? You mustn't concern yourself with my passions, Mr. Caburn. My mother-in-law was right. Why don't you go search out some real criminals?"

"Many a lonely woman has compromised her husband, Mrs. Nesmith." His voice had dropped to a soft pitch. "And I think that you are one very lonely woman."

She stalked to the door and yanked it open, ignoring the blast of chill air and snow. "I'm not lonely. But even if I was, it's neither a crime nor a sin. So scribble that down in your investigation if it makes you happy. Now get out and don't come back."

"I do have to be running along," he said, trailing behind her as he pulled his coat around him in an oddly cavalier fashion. "By the way, do you know exactly where your husband is right this minute?"

"Somewhere over the Atlantic," she snapped. "He's delivering a pouch to the American Embassy in Paris—direct to the embassy. If you're who you say you are, you should know that already."

"I do. I was just wondering if you did." He passed her at the door, pausing to glance from her feet to her head, his eyes stopping at the line of her breasts beneath the velvety rustling caftan.

"Your innuendo is very provocative," Anna flung at him, recoiling from his gaze. "But my husband is faithful to me and to his country, though I'm sure you find that corny. So why don't you go out and find someone else to check up on—like your own wife."

He paused at the bottom step and casually turned back. "I don't have a wife, Mrs. Nesmith. Haven't got any use for one."

Snow-filled wind molded the gown to her body, a seductive and revealing silhouette in the light cast from the foyer. A wisp of hair caught on her eyelashes. Anna brushed it out of her way, wanting to see the expression on his face, feeling an urgent need to thrust at him with a cutting verbal sword. "Of course you don't have a wife of your own," she said sweetly. "You use other men's wives, don't you?"

Caburn stared up at her, thinking she was a living canvas framed by the doorway, evocative and alluring. He felt his loins grow warm. His smile was genuine. "Well, you haven't said that *you* were faithful. Be seeing you, Mrs. Nesmith."

Anna backed into the house, slamming the door. She was angry at herself, at Kevin for not being home when she needed him, and at Francis Caburn for sniffing out her vulnerability. So, she was lonely. A lot of wives were. Right now was not the time to remember how often she had asked Kevin to find a job that would let him be home every night.

Falteringly she moved around the living room, touching this chair, that lamp, fluffing pillows, running her fingertips along the camelback sofa and the wing chairs she'd had upholstered in red-flowered chintz. Her eyes traveled to the golden oak conversation tables she had stripped and stained, to the antique floor lamps for which she had shopped and shopped just to find exactly the right shades, and the kilim rugs she had been lucky enough to purchase from a politician's wife—ex-wife now, she remembered. The entire room was out of kilter thanks to

Clara Alice, but it came in a flash of clarity that there was no imprint of Kevin in this house.

He had left only that morning, yet there were no magazines or books left open, no ties or sweaters flung on the back of a chair. He had no favorite chair, no special cup—what there was of her husband in their home was in his closet, three of the drawers in a chest in the bedroom and two shelves in the medicine cabinet. Her eyes darted around the room as Caburn's had, seeing as he must have seen. No hint of a man, no sports magazines, no pipes, no.... Everything reflected her own tastes, her likes, her wants. She swallowed and found her mouth dry.

A man, she thought, ought to leave behind something of himself, something to say he lived, breathed, touched and had passed that way. Absently she picked up the scarab Caburn had handled.

It was still faintly warm from his touch, the warmth like a talisman, reminding her that his presence lingered in the room as much as her husband's did not. She replaced it on the side table with a jerk, distraught that a stranger had left his imprint—one so tangible she could almost reach out and touch it.

She stood very still, thinking hard.

Caburn was strong, but she had her own strengths. It was his job to keep her off-balance, to make her succumb to doubt, to worry. All she had to do to get through this was to keep her thoughts in some bearable perspective.

"He's gone? Just like that?" Clara Alice asked as she shuffled into the room, her manner uncharacteristically subdued. She went to the foyer, making certain the door was closed and firmly locked. "What did he say? Is Kevin in trouble?"

Anna felt her color fading. "Can you think of any reason why he should be?"

Some of Clara Alice's familiar demeanor slipped into her expression. "Kevin has always been a good boy. A good son. And he's a good husband to you." She waved a fleshy hand in an arc. "Look how he's provided for us."

Anna looked—the sofa, the chairs, the tables, the lamps, the draperies—all had been purchased with money she had earned. For a moment it seemed to her that Clara Alice was on Caburn's side.

Her mind crept back reluctantly to the day Kevin had decided to buy the house. She had tried to talk him out of it. It had been frightening to see the rest of her money disappear into the down payment. Kevin had assured her it was an investment. It was. She was sure it was. She put out of her mind the shabbily genteel neighborhood in which it stood, and gave Clara Alice a weak smile. "Yes, Kevin is a good provider."

The older woman sniffed. "But, you're still acting like that man upset you."

"Am I?" Anna responded, unused to her mother-in-law making these kinds of sensitive observances. "Perhaps it's because Mr. Caburn is such a fierce-looking man. One doesn't expect to find his kind perched on a doorstep." She started pacing restlessly.

"He's out to get Kevin, isn't he? Get him fired?"

"No. I'm sure it was just as he said. Routine security check. You know these government types—if things are quiet they have to manufacture something to justify their jobs." Infallible instinct told Anna this wasn't the case with Caburn. He didn't appear to be a man who went looking for trouble where none existed. In trying to mollify Clara Alice she had only made more worry for herself. She tried to shake it off. "I'm sure Kevin knows about this. He just forgot to mention it, that's all. Security checks are quite ordinary for him. He probably never gave it a thought, and so forgot to tell us."

Clara Alice frowned, took a few steps in one direction, then another, and suddenly dropped down on her knees, her old bones creaking. "You'll never find it that way," she said, misinterpreting Anna's gliding around the room. She ran her fingers up and beneath the sofa skirt and the table legs, then stared intently into the lampshade nearest where Caburn had sat.

"I'm not looking for anything," Anna began, startled by her mother-in-law's actions.

"You should be. If we don't find them...."

"Find what? Have you lost something?"

"No, I'm looking for the bugs."

"Bugs? We don't have any bugs," Anna retorted, barely hiding her disgust.

"We might now," Clara Alice announced triumphantly. "Hidden microphones can be so tiny these days. Jack Anderson says—"

"Clara Alice!" Anna exclaimed hoarsely. "Please, get up from there." She felt a little sick.

"I was only trying to keep us safe," cried Clara Alice, shaking off Anna's hand. "We don't want anyone listening to us. That's an invasion of privacy."

Anna was shaken, but she thought that she was perhaps the world authority in the ways privacy could be invaded. After living with Clara Alice, a hidden microphone seemed mild. "I know," she managed, with just the right amount of concern. "Who's to say you aren't right? Let's eat now, shall we?"

Anna wasn't at all hungry, but there was something so normal, so ordinary about sitting at the old pine table, its patina richly polished from use. An everyday familiar ritual was what she needed to allay the foreboding that was beginning to cling to her thoughts like a tattered rag snagged on a nail.

She took her place at the table as mutely unhappy as before Caburn's visit, but with the added anguish of anxiety.

Later, as she lay in bed, each time she closed her eyes, thinking of Kevin, another face rose up to plague Anna. An angular face in which dark Tartar eyes tracked her every move, seemingly devouring her, mocking her, piercing her brain, so that all her secrets were laid bare for inspection.

She turned on the lamp, propping herself up on a pillow, forcing Caburn's visage from her mind and, until sleep overtook her, devised ways to reclaim the rapture in her marriage.

2

"Is CLARA ALICE UP YET?"

Anna, bundled up against the freezing air, was scraping ice from the windshield of her car. She turned at the sound of the voice of their nearest neighbor. Lila Hammond came barreling across her yard, wearing golashes, her dead husband's overcoat atop her nightgown and an aviator's hat with the flaps lowered over her ears. Anna smiled at the eccentric old woman. If only Clara Alice was as cheerful.

"She's up, Mrs. Hammond, and there's still plenty of coffee."

"Some weather, huh?" the widow observed. "Reminds me of the years Ace and I spent in the Arctic and those snowbound winters in...." She caught herself, her wrinkled cheeks flaring beyond the red of the cold. "I want to see if Clara will go to the movies with me tonight. My treat. See you."

"That would be lovely," Anna murmured, thinking that having the house to herself would be the opportunity she needed to return the living room to its proper order. Perhaps Kevin would be home today. Not that she was certain. He was sometimes so vague about his schedule, and she was reluctant to press him. Once, several months after they had been married, she had tried to pin him down. There was a concert she had wanted to attend. A shutter had come down over his vivid blue eyes, and he had told her she was never to question him about his work.

The windshield clear now, she began chipping at the ice on the door handle and, when the lock was clear, warmed her key with a match and inserted the key into the lock, pleased that it worked like a charm. But the car wouldn't start. She kept trying until the battery ran down. In the end she had to walk five blocks to the bus stop, and her day went downhill from there.

Two other employees didn't show up for work. The freak early-winter storm was taking its toll. The information center in which she worked was located in the old Madison building next door to the main library, and she *knew* the Library of Congress truly served the intellectual needs of the entire nation. She had watched the tour guides often enough, but their work wasn't the kind she had envisioned for herself.

She longed for a quiet cozy little bookstore with shelves and shelves of rare and not-so-rare books. A place to browse, a place to lose one's self in other worlds, other eras. Of course the nation's library offered all of that, but it didn't have her name over the door as proprietor. That was what she wished for most of all.

With information services shorthanded, the day passed swiftly and Anna had no time for troublesome thoughts. But she couldn't hold back a wistful sigh as she emerged onto 1st Street. The sky was dark, the smattering of snow swept away by the wind, leaving only frozen patches of ice, camouflaged by soot and dirt and odd bits of trash.

Washington's tour de force wasn't fashion, industry or big business. It was power. And the power makers were emerging from their offices, too, creating a mass of swaying bobbing energy. A line of tour buses was collecting its travelers in front of the Capitol. Anna snuggled down into the soft furry collar of her coat. She couldn't relate to power today.

She felt helpless and tired as she turned slowly toward the Metro. She missed her car.

"You look like you could use a friend."

It was impossible not to recognize that clear sardonic voice. "I don't," she told him pithily.

"An acquaintance of value, then?" he said, giving her a sideways smile.

"I won't commend you for sneaking up on me," she said, turning slightly to get Caburn in her line of view. He was wearing the same dark gray overcoat as last night, but had added a knitted muffler, draped over his broad shoulders, and an Irish tweed hat that had seen a lot of wear. He wore the brim cocked low over his right eye. She looked away from him, spending a good few seconds just trying to ignore the blood going hot in her veins, trying to ignore the airy feeling that was taking over her stomach. She glanced involuntarily at him again. "I know it may sound ungrateful of me, but there is nothing about our acquaintance I find valuable. Even a penny would be too much. Go find someone else to spy on."

He laughed, a low throaty intimate sound as if they were sharing a familiar private joke. "Had I been sneaking, you would never have spotted me. I was waiting for you."

"In your line of work it's the same thing." She didn't want to be near him. It brought to mind all the mixed emotions she had managed to suppress.

"I just want to talk."

Her lovely dark brows knitted together in a frown. "You want to do more than talk. You want to harrass me. Why investigate *me*? I don't have a job that requires any kind of clearance. Leave me alone."

She turned away, hurrying down the hill, picking up speed as she went and, as she neared the curb, slipped on a patch of ice. She went down with a surprised choking squeal, sprawling flat on her fanny. People turned to look, then moved on. An old man bent down as if to help her up. Anna brushed him away.

Four or five wonderfully caustic remarks came to Caburn's mind. An inner voice warned him against using them or behaving in any manner other than most sympathetic. Her skirt and coat had caught at her thighs. She had a presentable pair of legs. Very presentable. He felt his heart begin to pound unaccountably fast. He was seeing those legs lying beside his, seeing them wrapped around his muscular body.... He closed his eyes to blot out the vision, fighting the urge to stand there and let the picture continue. Instead, he picked up her purse, which had skidded near his foot. He held it out to her. "Maybe you don't need a friend as much as you do a guardian angel."

Anna was caught in the grip of pure mortification. She seemed not to know that she should pick herself up from the ground. She snatched the purse from Caburn's fingers, thrusting it under her arm. "I don't need you for a friend. I don't need you to guard me. I just want you to go."

Determined not to touch her, Caburn shoved his hands into his pockets as he leaned over, bending close, while a wave of pedestrians moved around them. "There are lots of ways to go about a security check, Mrs. Nesmith. You were assigned to me, so let's make the best of it, okay? I don't like this namby-pamby stuff—"

"Of course you don't! You'd rather be shooting guns, fighting with your fists—"

"Any more than you do. The sooner you begin cooperating, the faster we can get out of one another's lives. By the way, are you hurt?"

She gained her feet. "No." There was little she

could do to reinstate her dignity. Half of Washington had seen her fall, but she tried.

"Not having to see you again would suit me immensely. Why don't you make an appointment, like an insurance salesman? I'm off on Saturdays and Sundays. But I go to church on Sunday, most Sundays anyway, so that—"

His eyes narrowed to slits. "You want to make this hard on yourself? Go right ahead. I have all the time in the world. And stop behaving as though I'm asking you for a taste of sin. Your midwestern morality is safe with me."

"If I believed in violence, I'd slap you for that."

"Consider me slapped," he said thickly. Then, forgetting himself, he took her arm, propelling her down the street and around a wide corner despite her protests. "We'll talk now. My car is nearby."

His strides were long, athletic. Anna was hard put to keep the rest of her body even with the arm he was yanking on and watch where she put her feet at the same time, lest she take another inelegant spill. "I don't want to go anywhere with you. This is kidnapping. My mother-in-law is expecting me. She gets nervous if I'm not home on time."

"She's gone to the movies with Mrs. Hammond, that funny-looking creature who lives next door. You know it, I know it, so no excuses."

"You did do it!" gasped Anna. "Clara Alice was right! You did bug my house."

He choked back a vulgar epithet just in time. "May the saints preserve us. In case you didn't know, it takes a court order to install—"

"That wouldn't stop you. How *did* you get that information if not by eavesdropping?"

He stopped, twisting her around to face him, standing very close so that she became aware of his after-shave, a fresh clean lime scent. "The telephone," he ground out. "You could call it a listening device. If Alexander Bell knew that people like your mother-in-law were going to be abusing the things, he'd have kept them off the market. Your mother-in-law told me *without* prompting, that your car is frozen because dear overworked Nesmith forgot to put antifreeze in it, that she was going to the movies with Mrs. Hammond next door, that after pouring ketchup all over the nice roast she cooked for you last night, you didn't eat it, that you're mad at her for making just the *tiniest* adjustment to the living-room furniture...."

Anna's chin went up, her brown eyes going dark with anger. "Clara Alice seems to have been a fount of information. Perhaps you should ask her your questions."

He took a deep breath. "Give a man a break," he said, inhaling the scent of her, some flowery perfume that made him think of rolling hills and thick lush grass crushed beneath him. Her warm breath mingled with his, sending up a fine white mist in the cold air.

Their eyes met. Something sharp, something very private went between them. Anna's body began to shake. Every sensual nerve ending she possessed was affected, filling her with desire. There was an icy feeling in her stomach, but other parts, secret parts, were growing warm. Air rushed out of her lungs, an almost inaudible cry of dismay. She knew Caburn could see the want in her face, knew her lips were trembling. She closed her eyes and reminded herself that she had a husband. The dismay heightened as a wave of guilt washed over her.

"I want to go home," she said in a small husky voice.

"To dried-up roast beef?"

Caburn was shaken to his very core. He had felt

the electric current that had swept through them, taking him by surprise like a bolt of lightning. This wasn't something he had planned. This roaring in his head wasn't like anything he had ever experienced. The flu. He was coming down with the flu. He deserved it, standing around out here in the wind and snow like a fool. He sniffed experimentally, succeeding only in filling his nostrils with Anna's fragrance. He'd better watch it or he'd find himself getting reckless. He moved swiftly, covering the few feet to his car, unlocked the door and held it open.

Anna moved like a somnambulist, allowing him to usher her in as she struggled to get her thoughts together.

The car purred to life, its heater throwing out warmth, loosening aromas from the chill air. She picked out his after-shave, his soap, the odor of a sweet pipe tobacco and damp wool. It was completely dark now, the wind sharp, buffeting the car. She watched the headlights beaming on unfamiliar landmarks, too wracked with distress to ask him where he was taking her.

They had dinner in one of the small ethnic restaurants that flourish in Washington to the delight of homesick senators. Stuffed sausages with spicy red cabbage and frothy mugs of dark beer. Caburn ate while Anna stirred food around on her plate. She felt estranged from the world around her, from other diners, from the accordion music that seemed to come from nowhere, from Caburn. From herself.

"Something else?" he asked when she set her fork aside. It was the first effort he had made toward conversation throughout the past hour.

Anna answered him absently.

He signaled the waiter to bring coffee. "That's it then. Let's get down to business." His tone had a cruel edge to it. She watched his expression change from ambivalence to anticipation.

He wants to trap me, she thought. This whole affair centered around Kevin, and Kevin was just an ordinary man...not to her, but to the government. Only the thick black attaché case he carried was extraordinary for what it contained. She had an idea, one that terrified her, but then everything that was happening would make sense.

"Has Kevin been kidnapped by some terrorist organization? Have they got him and you're keeping it a secret because of the documents he was carrying? Please! I've got to know if he's safe."

He stared at her long and hard out of his flat gray eyes, hidden now beneath lowered lids. "You're letting your imagination get carried away. This is a routine investigation."

"Is it routine for you to come to my home? To be waiting on me after work? To take me to dinner? Routine is when Kevin filled out *reams and reams* of background forms when he was hired two years ago."

"One, we have to eat and I was hungry. Two, I don't do the reasoning out. I'm asking you standard questions. It's my job to doubt everything."

"Well, do you have to look at me like you do? You're making me feel so...so exposed."

His eyes left her, traveled around the room, came back. "Don't make me pick this out of you. I want to know about your life, how and where you met Nesmith. What you've been doing since you moved to Washington. Are there any unexplained absences from home? Other women? Do you have any foreigners for friends?"

The hair on Anna's neck rose in alarm. "Are you questioning Kevin's loyalty to the United States?"

He leaned forward, grinding out, "Will you please

stop answering my questions with questions? We'll
be at it all night. I have a date later, so—"

A date. She felt a stab of emotion, stark and cold.
"Whatever you say." She shrugged with indifference. "I met Kevin when he was a student at the
University of Kansas. I was an assistant librarian
there. He was just out of the army, going to college
on the GI bill while waiting for an opening at the
Department of State. We met and married."

She had been worried that she would never
marry. Never find a husband. At thirty, as she had
been then, women worried, she recalled glumly.

"First marriage for both of you?"

Anna nodded. "Kevin lived with his mother in
Shawnee Mission, and I with my dad. A few months
after we were married, Kevin got his interview in
Washington and was hired. We haven't made a lot
of friends. He travels too much to make any plans."

"It's expensive to buy a home in D.C. How'd you
manage that?"

"I—we used my savings. I'd been working for
eight years."

"He didn't mind that? Using your money?"

Anna bristled. "It was *our* money after we married. We share everything."

That's not true, she thought. *Kevin keeps a part of
himself from me. He always has.* But she had learned to
live with his moody silences. He loved her; that was
all that mattered. She was safe. Secure. Wanted.

"What about sexual habits? Anything funny or
strange? Does he ask you to do anything peculiar in
bed that you've refused?"

Anna reeled as though struck. "This is awful.
How can you ask me such things?"

His jaw jerked tight, his eyes narrowing to slits,
though his gaze never wavered from her face. "Make
it easy for both of us."

"Easy?" Her eyes flashed and her chin went up. "You must have a deplorable paucity of sexual experiences to have to ask questions like that."

"I get my share," he said grimly.

"Good for you. My sex life is private. You're a voyeur, that's what you are."

"Does that mean: no, you won't answer... no, he wants nothing peculiar... or no, you don't refuse anything he asks of you?"

She folded her arms and leaned back in her chair. "I'm not answering any more of your questions."

He emitted a ragged sigh. "Yes, you will," he promised, and signaled for the waiter to bring their check. "But let's leave it for today. I've had enough. C'mon, I'll take you home."

"I don't like you, Caburn."

"That'll pass for an understatement," he muttered and took her arm, ushering her out of the restaurant and to his car.

Anna huddled on the seat, vacillating between fits of anguish and anger. On one hand she was worried about this routine security check that was beginning to sound as though it wasn't, and on the other she was furious that Caburn felt so at ease asking her such... *nasty* questions, which he truly expected her to answer. If only she could be certain of what had provoked this inquiry. She couldn't believe that Kevin had done anything against his country. He believed in freedom and he loved his job—too much so, she thought wryly. And then it came to her. The Summit talks were coming up. That was it, she breathed with silent relief. Kevin was being given a thorough going-over. After all, couriers were often in the presence of heads of state, and governments were paranoid about their safety, often with good reason. There was a dangerous element about Kevin's work, too. The documents he carried were valuable, sometimes so secret that he traveled with a surreptitious bodyguard.

Still, doubts began to nibble at her. Tormenting doubts. Questions Caburn had asked and slanted toward her personal life, her finances. Somehow he made everything sound and seem so sordid. Not only that, Caburn made it seem as though she wasn't...wasn't paying attention to what was going on in her life, in her marriage—made it seem that she was looking at life through the proverbial rose-tinted glasses. But she wasn't. At least she didn't think she was. She had learned long ago when her parents were together that if things were going along nicely, one should not ask questions that might start up a row. Anna felt she was like most people she knew—she didn't like to face conflicts. She didn't like how she was feeling now, either.

She glanced at Caburn. The car was dark, but his profile was lifted from shadows by an occasional streetlamp. She could see his brow furrowed in a frown, see his taut jaw and the wiry curls that slipped from beneath the brim of his hat. His attention seemed given over to handling the car, to the oncoming traffic, the slick roads, but in the mesmerized manner of one whose mind wanders when on a stretch of a long familiar highway.

She wondered what his personal life was like. She wondered how he would feel if a man such as himself was asking questions of his wife, especially the sort of questions he'd been asking *her*. But Caburn didn't have a wife. Suddenly she wanted to know more about him, know *everything* about him, and she felt that stark stabbing emotion unleash itself once again.

"Have you ever been married?" she asked, struggling to arrange her features into an expression of casual interest in case he looked her way. She didn't want him to misconstrue curiosity for affection.

His fingers tensed on the steering column and his lips thinned. "Almost—once," he said harshly, so that she felt constrained to bungle on.

"I don't see why you should go all cold and stiff lipped just because I ask you a simple question. You shouldn't mind if I pry—you make a living at it."

"There's a difference." His voice was grainy and he didn't look at her.

Anna leaned back and closed her eyes. Tears were stirring behind her lids and she didn't know why.

Suddenly Caburn's hand covered hers, a strong hand topped with tiny tufts of blond hair. It felt warm as he squeezed gently. "Stop worrying. I can feel you doing it."

His unexpected compassion nearly did her in. A sob caught at the back of her throat. "I just wish Kevin would hurry home."

He moved his hand back to the steering column. "I know you do."

"You don't know!" she exclaimed in a guilty way, realizing that Caburn was in her mind in a way no man other than her husband should be. "How could you? How can you know what I'm thinking, what I'm feeling...?" *It was your face that kept coming to me last night, not Kevin's. I fantasized about you, and oh, I can't seem to help myself.* It wasn't as if he was an actor separated from her world by television or a movie screen or a gossip column. He was too real, too alive...too close. She shifted away from him in her mind and in the car, putting more space between them.

"You're not planning on doing something foolish, are you?" he asked. "Like opening the door and jumping out?" He had begun slowing down the moment he caught her movement.

She shook her head. "I'm just making myself comfortable."

Caburn knew it wasn't true. He thought it a very telling remark.

Anna sat stiffly after the car came to a halt at the curb in front of her house while Caburn went around to open her door. As she stepped out she slipped again, and by an instinctive reflex drilled into him, Caburn's hand shot out, righting her. Her cheek grazed his. Even through the thick fabric of her coat, his touch was electric, his grip firm, so that she had to suppress the gasp that rose from within. Caburn jerked his hand away as if he'd touched a live coal.

She choked out a thank you, averting her face, avoiding eye contact. She wanted suddenly to confess to Caburn the irrational feeling of joy she had experienced at his touch, to tell him that she welcomed it. Tell him, too, that it was a wish beyond all propriety. She watched her footing as she walked up the sidewalk.

She sensed Caburn behind her, knew he had stopped as she went up the steps to the stoop.

"You're a very loyal lady, Anna, perhaps too loyal." There was a tightness in his throat that would not be explained away by flu or cold.

There it was again, Anna thought, that way he had of speaking to her that made suspicion leap into her mind. If only she could exorcise this awful doubt. She turned back to him slowly, her soft patrician chin going up, revealing tawny hollows that had been hidden by her collar. "What do you mean? Please... what's this all about—really?"

His expression went incredibly grim. "Forget it. I spoke out of turn."

"But—"

"Good night, Anna. Pleasant dreams."

"*Pleasant dreams?*" She swallowed hard. "You're a cruel man. There's nothing good about you—nothing." She had to make herself believe that. She had to blot out those moments he had showed such compassion. And as she stepped into the house and closed the door behind her, leaving him, she was terrified that she would never see him again.

Caburn returned to his car, watching and waiting until Anna had unlocked the door of her house and disappeared into its depths. Then he did something that would have astonished his chief. He pounded on the steering wheel like a madman, muttering a series of violent expressive curses.

3

ALBERT PHIPPS WAS TAKING his time filling his pipe, tamping the tobacco, seemingly absorbed in putting flame to the bowl. He smoked an acrid, foul-smelling tobacco and Caburn knew he'd be lighting up soon himself in self-defense. He winced as a cloud of smoke wafted his way. Phipps noticed and grinned. "Not all of us are so lucky and so rich we can order up special blends from New York and London."

Caburn squirmed inwardly. It made him uncomfortable for anyone to mention his wealth. Phipps knew it and did it on purpose, yet his words were backhanded camaraderie with no sting.

When he had first come under Phipps's scrutiny, the wheat farm he owned and the running of it had been discussed. Once the security chief was satisfied that it would in no way interfere with Caburn's work, he viewed his colleague's bank balance with equanimity, counting it as a plus. It gave at least one of his field officers entry into a level of society for which few of them were equipped. Phipps had a mandate to keep his country safe from within and he did. Treason, he said, could worm its way into all social strata.

Shifting his weight in the old leather chair to avoid the loose spring, Caburn waited, his eyes hooded but trained on his boss. Hardly anyone meeting Phipps for the first time suspected the force that drove him, and he didn't seem a man to fear. He was as ugly as homemade sin, or worse, and knew it. His Adam's apple bobbed in a scrawny neck that seemed far too weak for the powerful head that it held. Caburn knew though that there was nothing weak about Phipps. He had a mind like a steel trap, and his casual, sometimes stumbling way often set his prey at such ease that the quarry would be astonished when Phipps closed in.

They had worked together for nine years now and Caburn had seen him shaken only once—when Phipps's wife, Louise, a former beauty queen, had shot him in the leg in a fit of domestic jealousy. Phipps had made two acidic comments about the incident: "Who'd a thought it?" he had said with a sense of wonder the day he emerged from the hospital on crutches; and later, when he was ensconced behind the gray metal desk, he had spoken with a kind of inverted pride. "You'll notice that Louise took great care where she aimed." But now, his rheumy eyes held a deadly calculating look as he squinted through a cloud of smoke. "Well...any luck?"

"I canvassed the neighbors. All say the Nesmiths are a cozy couple."

Phipps frowned. "Couldn't a been too cozy or we wouldn't have this mess to clean up. What about the Nesmith woman—think she has a clue?"

"Not so far as I can tell, but I don't think the marriage is all that firm." Caburn didn't want it to be. He was a man with morals. He couldn't come between a man and his wife, but if there was already trouble, already a breach....

"What does she know?" Phipps said, interrupting Caburn's reverie.

Caburn shrugged, crossing his legs. "She knows he was delivering direct to the embassy. I think that means she's aware of the Armed Forces Center at Orly and that Nesmith bypasses it."

"Well, that's neither here nor there now," Phipps said glumly, taking up a pencil nub and making a note in the file before him. "How does she strike you?"

Caburn started, his heart and his head pounding in different rhythms. "How does who strike me?"

"The Nesmith woman. Who in hell do you think I'm talking about—the First Lady?" Leaning forward, Phipps rested his bony elbows on the desk, stabbing in Caburn's direction with his pipe. "What's got into you lately? You're as cross as an arse-shot grizzly. I want to know how the Nesmith woman strikes you. Impressions. You do have an impression, don't you?" Suddenly Phipps's old eyes went wide and he leaned back in his chair. "Caburn! I never thought I'd see the day—you're blushing."

"We've been friends a long time, Phipps..." Caburn said, his brooding Tartar eyes narrowing. But he stopped the warning the moment it sprang to his lips. He'd been surprised, just as Phipps expected him to be. Cursing himself, he took out his pipe, his tobacco pouch, filled his pipe and took his time lighting it, testing the draw. Then he permitted himself a smile. "She's nice, that's how she strikes me."

Phipps emitted an expletive. "What in hell does *nice* mean? Give it to me. Stop this dancing around."

"She goes to work every day at the Library of Congress, clips stuff out of magazines, takes care of Nesmith's mother, a clinging vine type."

"Who? The mother or the wife?"

"The mother," Caburn said, shifting to avoid a loose spring in the old chair.

Phipps drew hard on his pipe. "What's the house like? Money?"

"No money. It's old—average, clean. Furniture's secondhand but elegant. Black-and-white television.

Everything tastefully done. She dresses well. They used her money for the down payment."

Now Phipps was drumming his fingers on the desk. That always irritated Caburn. He knew his boss was cataloging questions, trying to find answers. "You think Nesmith pulled this stunt just to get out from under his mother's thumb?"

"His mother's maybe," Caburn said slowly, shaking his head. He was remembering the feel of Anna's trembling hand beneath his, the slight touch of her cheek when she fell against him. "Can't see him doing this to Anna."

"Oh? Anna, is it?" Phipps repeated, drawing long on the syllables of the name. "She's a looker then, not your usual stereotyped librarian?"

Caburn's dark piercing eyes took on a preoccupied look. He wouldn't be drawn into a trap a second time. "Fair," he commented nonchalantly, knowing he was doing Anna a disservice.

Phipps relit his pipe, took a long puff and looked at Caburn carefully. "I know what you're like around the ladies, so you watch your step here. I'm not ordering you to stay out of her bed, but I'm warning you— when these women start their caterwauling I don't want any fallout in my department."

Caburn shot out of his chair. A move that was fast, athletic and meant to frighten. Phipps didn't move, didn't speak, but one of his bushy gray eyebrows worked furiously as he watched Caburn stalk the room, empty his pipe, jam it back into his pocket and finally slump back into his chair.

"Damn Nesmith to hell, anyway, Phipps. Pull me off this case. Put me onto something else."

There was a heavy silence between them while Phipps's fingers drummed incessantly on the metal desk. Then he stopped and pulled out a folder from a drawer, placing it on his desk before opening it. He absorbed himself in it for several seconds. "There's an aide to one of our department heads whose spending has come off a bit flashy in recent weeks. He hasn't had an inheritance, hasn't won the football pool in a year and his wife doesn't work. He's suddenly taken up an expensive hobby. The rub is that he has access to codes. Interest you?"

Caburn flinched inwardly, suspecting that agreement was coming too easily, too quickly. "Fine with me," he said.

"This hobby group is a tight bunch of fellows— daredevils, I'd say. But the hobby group would be your best bet to penetrate. And you can afford it," he added slyly.

"I'll take it." Danger would suit him well right now, Caburn decided. Anything to work off this kinetic energy he had been trying to stifle.

"Let me see..." mumbled Phipps, dropping his gaze to the folder once more. "This guy's a skydiver."

Caburn whitened. "Damn you," he said thickly. "That's below the belt."

Phipps gave him an avuncular smile. "Ain't it though?" He put the file away, slamming the drawer shut. "Now you listen to me, Francis Caburn. You stay with the Nesmith woman, and you stay tight. Like a leech. That's an order. This is a damned delicate situation and she's pivotal. I want her kept calm... smooth like glass. Allay her every concern. Move in with her if you have to."

"The mother-in-law would drive me up the wall."

"Ah! Why should you be different? The experience won't hurt you. Sooner or later you'll have one of your own, and I pity you there. You'll be nothing but raw putty. Now, get out of here. Louise has supper waiting. You know it's not healthy for me to be late." Phipps got up, followed Caburn to the door, limping slightly. "Oh, hold on a minute. Got a personal message for you here someplace." He went back to his desk, rummaged through a ream of loose papers. "From your stepdad."

Caburn took the message, read it, crumpled it into a ball and shoved it into his pocket. Phipps thought he could read the rage in Caburn's gray eyes. "Things not going well back home?" he asked.

"Same old thing," Caburn answered, brooding. "He wants to mortgage the farm to buy tractors with air-conditioned cabs, lease more land...." His voice trailed off. His stepfather had been trying to wrest the farm from him since Caburn had taken it over when he'd turned twenty-one. From the time Caburn was six until he had reached his majority, his stepfather had counted the farm his own. Though he didn't live there, Caburn felt the farm to be a link with his ancestors, burly pioneers who had settled the plains. It was a heritage he expected to keep intact for his own sons. He snapped back to the present when he realized Phipps had been speaking to him.

"Remember, constant surveillance on this Nesmith thing."

Caburn nodded absently as he stepped into the elevator that would take him from the bowels of the building. *Constant surveillance.* The words worked their way around in Caburn's brain and hung there. *Watch Anna Nesmith.* In the time they had shared, he hadn't been able to tear his eyes away since she had surprised him with that curious question on her doorstep. It was a question that didn't get asked— ever—in his line of work. He had to give her credit for grit.

He hoped she had a lot more.

He fingered his mustache. She had intimated that

he looked menacing. Had called him cruel. As he stepped from the building into the cold dark evening he began to wonder how he could improve his image.

AN EARLY-MORNING FOG draped its misty white shroud over Washington. Anna pulled the green window coverings back and looked out. She couldn't help it—she wanted to see if Caburn was lurking around, but she couldn't see beyond the shrubbery that brushed against the window. At least, she thought, it had stopped sleeting. She could hear the steady drip from the eaves of the house as ice melted. Today, finally, Washington would be coming out from under the freak winter storm.

She had to ride the Metro again that morning, and found herself searching among faces at every stop for Caburn. She had a crazy notion that she would merely have to turn in her seat, glance over her shoulder, and there he would be.

When she left the library after work, she again scouted for him surreptitiously as she pulled on her gloves. If he was nearby he didn't make himself known.

She joined the masses pouring out of various government buildings for the rush homeward, refusing to admit her disappointment that Caburn had not been waiting for her. Thinking of him made her nerves chaotic. In less than forty-eight hours Caburn had become a presence in her life. Like Clara Alice. An irritant. He only had an effect on her because of Kevin. He had no affect on her personally. None at all.

Yet on the bus home her brow was furrowed in a

continuous frown. She kept repeating to herself: *Kevin is my husband. I love him and he loves me* ... over and over, and inside she had a horrible empty feeling ... and still Caburn's face would not sink into oblivion.

As she rounded the corner of the block on which she lived, Anna saw that the hood was up on her car. She stopped and closed her eyes. Thank God! Kevin was home. Fixing her car. She was safe. She picked up her pace, and as she came closer, her steps faltered. That wasn't Kevin's dark head beneath the hood. That wasn't his lean rangy body in old Levi's and a plaid flannel shirt with the tail hanging out. It was a blond head, belonging to a thick powerful body. Curiously, her heart raced and blood thundered against her temples even as her feet slowed.

"Just what do you think you're doing?" she sputtered with just the right amount of righteous indignation.

He backed out from beneath the raised hood. "You're lucky the block and radiator on this rattletrap weren't frozen solid and split, or you'd need a new motor. I've finally gotten the water warmed and drained and filled the radiator with antifreeze. I'll charge up the battery with my car—"

"This is too much." Her mouth was suddenly dry. "Is this part of your investigation, too? My husband will be home today, perhaps tomorrow. He would've done this. You had no right...." She heard herself babbling and bit her lip, coming to a grinding halt. Caburn's proximity intimidated her. She gave a bitter thought to Kevin for leaving her so vulnerable.

Slowly, as if it was a ritual he performed every day, Caburn wiped his hands on a piece of old towel. Anna's attention was riveted to his hands. They had touched her yesterday, squeezing gently, compassionately, but now she thought them dangerous. Judas's hands.

"Nesmith's been delayed," he said. His head down, he was absorbed in cleaning grease from his fingers so that his expression was unreadable.

Anna went hot and cold. "Delayed?" she repeated, desolated, biting her lower lip so that her voice lost its volume. "Arrested?" That was her worst fear, and she hated herself for having to ask, hated herself for doubting Kevin, and hated Caburn for making it necessary. He was turning her inside out so that her entire being was laid bare to him.

His head came up and he studied her at length. "No, not arrested," he said calmly. He knew now that he had raised some suspicion. "There was an American legation in Paris on its way to Beirut. Nesmith was assigned to it. You know the Syrians still haven't withdrawn their troops from Lebanon."

"But why? Why Kevin?"

"He was there, available, and has the right security clearance." Caburn felt the bile rising in his throat at this blatant lie. Damn Albert Phipps to hell and back for keeping him on this case.

"For . . . for how long?" There was such a bruising pleading in Anna's voice that Caburn had to turn away.

"How the hell should I know?" he muttered. He hadn't felt so miserable doing something he knew he had to do since he had told his mother he was leaving the farm because he couldn't put up with his stepdad another day. "I don't make policy. I was just told to give you the message."

"Do you have to keep hanging around?" she asked him brokenly, her hand fluttering in an aimless gesture.

"I'm afraid so."

Anna stood there a moment, taking in his broad

strength, his burning gray eyes, the line of his jaw, taut now with tension, and abruptly something inside her snapped. "All right. You gave me the message. Were you also told to repair my car?"

"No. I'm doing it on my own—"

"For some reason, the good Samaritan image doesn't fit you," she said, obsessed with the urge to hurt him as she was hurting, to penetrate his cool exterior. She needed to know all his flaws; she needed to dislike him. To do one kind thing for her was so very unjust of him.

"Maybe not, but you're assigned to me and I don't like riding buses or following in their exhaust." He gave her a teasing smile. "I'm just trying to make my job easier, that's all."

"I'm not going to break any laws." *I'm not going to commit adultery.* "So you're wasting your time."

The sunlight was weak on Anna's face, but Caburn was seeing her as she would look on canvas. An artist would have to use lots of light and shadows to catch her oval beauty, to show the intense depth in her brown eyes. "No, I don't expect that you will, Anna Nesmith..." he said darkly. "Either man's or God's." He told himself he didn't care.

"Anna!"

Clara Alice was all commotion on the stoop. An overnight case was plopped at her feet; her brown cotton stockings were wrinkled down around her ankles. She wore an old cloth coat and her gray hair, usually so primly kept, was flyaway, a sure sign she was agitated. "I'm leaving!" she shouted.

Anna's mouth dropped open in mortification. "You're what? Where? You can't leave—you can't go anywhere dressed like that. What's going on?" She turned back to Caburn. "You! You had something to do with this!"

He shook his head. "Not me. I don't involve myself in domestic arguments. Worldwide predicaments are more my line." He sent up a tiny silent prayer that the old woman wasn't bluffing.

But Clara Alice was so full of anger that her face was actually purple. She came shuffling down the sidewalk, the suitcase bumping against her knees. Anna's heart contracted.

"You don't want me here," Clara Alice accused Anna. "I've known it all along. You changed the furniture back last night before I got home from the movies. You do it all the time to spite me. I'm...I'm useless here. And another thing! It's not Kevin's fault that I don't have grandchildren. You're barren, that's what! I'm staying with Lila until Kevin gets home and straightens you out, then I'll come home—not a minute before!"

Anna was struck speechless, devastated that Clara Alice had aired such private personal remarks so publicly. Her face flamed as Clara Alice stalked past.

Lila Hammond came out of her house, loping across her yard, skirting patches of slick mud. She sidled up to Anna, patting her arm. "Don't worry, dear. I'll calm Clara down, maybe even talk some sense into her. I could teach her to drive or something, get her mind off herself."

Anna couldn't take it all in. She glanced wildly around, noting Caburn, his face inscrutable as he leaned on the car; a neighbor across the street stepped out onto his porch. Finally her gaze returned to Lila Hammond. "Drive?" she said stupidly. "In Washington?"

Lila was watching Clara Alice disappear into her home, missing the distress in Anna's expression. "I've been thinking about motoring down to my place on St. Simons Island off the coast of Georgia. Clara Alice would be company. Would you mind?"

The meaning of her words took a moment to register with Anna. "Lila, that would be a godsend, but Clara's a handful even on her best days. ..."

"I once helped Ace wrestle a walrus to get its tusks. Clara Alice can't be much worse," she laughed and turned to go. "I'll keep you posted." Her departing wave included Caburn.

In the space of a heartbeat silence descended upon the tree-lined street. The wind soughed and there was the muted sound of traffic on the main boulevard some blocks away. Anna had a strange feeling that she had just participated in a poorly acted drama, that the curtain had rung down in the middle of the first act and left her standing there, with words yet to be spoken, actions yet to be carried out, a rushing climax unreached.

She discovered Caburn watching her, caressing her with his eyes. She opened her mouth to speak, but no words came. Suddenly she bolted for the haven of her home, charging through her front door, locking it behind her. She kicked off her shoes in the foyer, then made her way into the kitchen where she took two aspirins, washing them down with a deep gulp of brandy that made her eyes water.

She fought the tears as the brandy warmed her, soothed her and gave her false courage. She wouldn't give in to self-pity. That was Clara Alice's domain. She told herself to look on the bright side. For months now she had longed for privacy and solitude. She had it, for tonight anyway. Pity Lila Hammond. She was the one having to tolerate Clara Alice, who probably wouldn't wind down for hours. ... And pity Clara Alice, too, who was old and scared and didn't want to be alone. But Anna determined she could never, ever forgive Clara Alice for that outburst about grandchildren. She felt as though her soul had been sliced in two.

Solitude had a calming effect on her as much as the brandy and aspirins. She took a fragrant bath, brushed her hair until it gleamed, examined with disgust the dark circles beneath her eyes and refused to let her mind dwell on any unpleasantness. She wasn't really hungry, but having her tiny kitchen to herself for the first time in a year had a certain appeal. She puttered around until she had prepared a pot of tea, cold roast beef with horseradish, a boiled potato and a hot roll. She put it all on a tray and took it into the front room, passing the chair that faced front. She didn't allow herself to glance out the bay windows to see if Francis Caburn was still outside. She told herself that she didn't care if he sat out there all night and froze.

It was when she bent to place her tray on the coffee table that she saw him in the chair, his booted foot swinging casually to his own inner rhythm. She snapped a look into his face. "How did you get in here?"

He held up her key ring. "House key's on this. You were right about the layout of this furniture. It looks better this way."

Anna contemplated him for a moment. He did not take his eyes from her, and she could feel them devouring her. Unconsciously she retied the sash on her robe, a protective gesture, fighting the pull of him in the only way she knew how. "Get out," she said. Her heart was pounding so fast she heard it thudding in her ears.

Caburn didn't budge as his eyes dropped to her plate. "Got enough for two?"

Anna leapt to her feet, alert, like a doe ready to spring to safety. "No. Go find someone else to cook your dinner. You said you didn't have any use for a wife, so quit trying to make use of me." She knew at once her choice retort was utterly wrong.

He smiled and for an instant there was warmth in his slate-gray eyes. More than warmth—a passion held in check. "Cooking wouldn't be the first use I'd make of you, dear Anna Nesmith, but right now I'm hungry. If an old stray came around to rake leaves or shovel snow, you'd feed him, wouldn't you? I've been working in the cold for three hours on your car. Won't that buy my dinner?" The smile was lingering in the lines around his eyes.

Against her will, she felt herself giving in. "You're trying to make me feel guilty."

"Do you?"

She bent over and with one delicately tapered finger shoved the tray toward him. "Here. Eat. Does that answer your question?"

"Now you're doing it. Making me feel contrite... or," he continued softly, "do you enjoy playing the martyr?"

Anna's head lifted in that regal way that Caburn was coming to watch for—her body language gave him more information than any of her words ever could. "Sticks and stones can break my bones—" she began.

"And words can break spirits," he snapped, his voice tinged with a raspy quality that indicated he could be dangerous if enraged. "What is it about you that makes it so easy for us to argue two minutes into a conversation?"

"Maybe we don't like one another. Did you ever give that a thought?" Her legs were going weak now. She slipped into the wing chair, making the move as graceful and as casual as she could. Her robe gaped open, revealing a long shapely leg and part of a creamy thigh. She caught Caburn's eyes sliding there, and flicked the robe closed. "Same as yesterday," she snapped, glowering at him. "A voyeur."

"You're deliberately needling me," he accused, letting his annoyance show. "I don't like it, Anna. I know my work interrupts lives, but I didn't divide the world into the good guys and the bad guys. My job is to make sure the bad, and you'd be surprised, the good, too, don't compromise this nation."

"How patriotic."

"Yes, it is patriotism. I won't apologize for it. I wish I had never stepped onto your staid and cozy little corner of earth, but I have. I was ordered to, so don't patronize me."

Anna frowned and looked away. "Patriotism doesn't excuse bad manners. Sneaking up on me all the time, barreling your way into my home, frightening me... and... and other things...." She couldn't go on because every cell in her body, every nerve ending was aware of him, responding to him. Her heart beat faster, her lips parted, her breathing went shallow and she knew it was wrong. She closed her eyes to blot him from her sight.

"What other things?" he asked softly. She kept her eyes closed, refusing to answer. "Anna, do you love Kevin Nesmith?"

Her hands came up to cover her face. "I think I do. I know I do. It's just that you're confusing me." Her voice was muffled, a sob building at the back of her throat. She swallowed it and lifted her face. "Why do you have to do this? Everything was going so well until you showed up."

"Was it?" he said coldly.

"Yes! Yes! Yes!" she erupted with fury, beating her fists on the chair arms for emphasis. "We have problems like any other couple—but you keep making me think something terrible is happening! You're making me see shadows and doubts where there aren't any." She glared at him, her brown eyes wide, filled with emotion. "I can *feel* that you want something to be wrong here. You...you feed on other people's problems. I could tell that the moment I opened the door to you. Oh, I wish that I had slammed it in your face. I wish I had never let you in...."

"You would've had to talk to me sooner or later. You've got to learn to face facts."

"Facts? What facts?"

"I can't tell you."

"See? See what I mean? You're scaring me. You're not married, so you can't know what an important thing marriage is...."

"Tell me," he prompted.

"You wouldn't understand. It's...it's being there when the other person needs you. It's knowing what the other is thinking and feeling without words. It's being safe."

"You think *I* mean you harm? Don't you feel safe with me?"

She closed her eyes and let her head fall back against the chair. "No." It was a whisper of a word signaling a boundary that she must never approach, a mental chalk mark over which she must never cross.

Caburn quelled the next question that rose in his mind. With her head thrown back, Anna's neck was left vulnerable, revealing pulsating veins in delicate hollows. Her lashes were thick and feathery lying along her cheek, fluttering now and again in motion with whatever thoughts were forging into her brain. He felt his mouth going dry, as if all the juices had been sucked out of him.

He knew what he looked like—not handsome, but there was something about his scarred, nicked-up body that attracted women—all women, married or not. He had never had one tell him she didn't feel safe with him. Anna's no struck at his ego like a sharp hot knife. He felt a stirring within him that made his heart act oddly, as if it were trying to pound its way out of his chest.

Suddenly, without warning, the facets of the investigation surged into his mind, its labyrinth a maze of truths, each of which Anna Nesmith would have to face, have to absorb, have to suffer. His face tightened, and at length, when Anna didn't stir, he stood up and started for the door.

"Caburn?" Her eyes were huge and brown and liquid in her face.

He hesitated, turning only halfway to look back at her. His expression was both grave and savage.

Anna took a deep shaky breath and said, "Please, don't come back."

He looked at her, pressing her image into his mind. "I have to."

After the door closed Anna just sat there, her mind in a turmoil. She could not think straight. A clock on a small table in the hall struck the half hour; a mournful hollow chime in the deceptive silence. It felt as though it were coming from within her soul.

5

It was just before dawn when Anna dragged herself out of bed the following morning. She had spent a miserable night, sleep coming only in snatches, and each time she had closed her eyes there was the terrifying specter of Caburn. He would not budge from behind her lids, would not make room for Kevin. Over and over she envisioned the first time Caburn had knocked on her door, always changing the scenario....

Mentally she opened the door and saw a short, fat, baldheaded man wearing a gray overcoat.

"Mrs. Nesmith?"

"Yes?"

"We're doing routine security checks on State Department couriers. For safety reasons."

"Of course. Come in."

More than once she would open the door to see a blond man wearing a gray overcoat.

"Mrs. Nesmith?"

"Yes?"

"I'm from State. We're doing routine security checks on our couriers."

"Just a moment, I'll call my husband."

Or:

"Mrs. Nesmith?"

"Yes?"

"I'm from State. We're doing routine security checks on our couriers."

"Kevin had his this morning before he left for France."

"Oh. Sorry to disturb you. Goodbye."

Anna could dream all she wanted, but when she opened her eyes and turned on the light, reality crowded out that fantasy. Nothing was changed. She had let Caburn in and had been sucked up into his powerful aura. The Renoir print on the wall no longer pictured unknown dancers, but herself and Caburn. When she saw herself lying on the chaise longue, it was Caburn's muscular body coming toward her. Anna swelled with guilt.

Fully awake, she had more control. She was able to loathe Caburn and what he was doing to her, doing to her marriage. Exercising constant control over her thoughts made her head throb unmercifully, making her feel lost and out of step with her usual placid way of life.

As she dressed for work that morning, she glimpsed herself in the mirror hung behind the bedroom door. She was shocked. Her cheeks looked hollow as they never had, her dark eyes seemingly swallowed up in her face.

Later she had readied the coffeepot and forgotten to plug it in, cracked an egg into an unoiled frying pan, and gone into Clara Alice's room to wake her, remembering only then, as she stared at the empty bed, that Clara Alice was visiting Lila Hammond.

An hour passed and it was still too early to leave for work. She stepped outside to retrieve the *Washington Post* and found it was Saturday. She didn't have to work.

Laugh! she commanded herself.

She felt like crying.

She plugged in the coffeepot, took off her working clothes, replacing them with the white velour caftan and, taking the newspapers, sat at the tiny breakfast nook in the kitchen. She sipped coffee and scanned the papers to see what was happening in Lebanon. If the peace legation was tossed out, Kevin would be home at once.

Marines were being sent in. Unofficially. Whatever that meant. However, if the situation escalated, military couriers would be brought in to replace Kevin.

No other news held her attention. Anna was restless, unable to submerge herself in print of any kind. She tossed the papers aside and began to putter around the house. In the master bedroom her glance lingered on the twin beds. How she hated them.

KEVIN HAD HAD SOME PRESSING business the weekend Clara Alice was to be released from the hospital in Kansas City where she'd been rushed by ambulance after suffering a mild stroke. It had fallen to Anna to fly out, check Clara Alice out of the hospital, and close up her mother-in-law's house. It had been at Kevin's insistence, too, that Clara Alice be moved to Washington. Then, Anna hadn't minded. She thought it was admirable that Kevin was devoted to his mother. That was before she knew Clara Alice so well. That was before Clara Alice had walked into the spare room in which she was to sleep, and turned her "pity-me" look on Kevin.

"Oh, darling, you know I can't abide a single bed. I toss and turn so. Your father was always complaining...and they remind me of the hospital. We can't push them together, they always slide apart. I'll end up falling out of bed and my old bones...."

Anna had thought Clara Alice's old bones were too well padded to break even if she'd fallen out a third-story window. Though she was exhausted from the whirlwind trip to Kansas City, Anna had helped Kevin move their great double bed into the spare room and she and Kevin had taken the singles. "It's only temporary," Kevin had said. Three months later she broached the subject of buying another bed. "Mother's hospital bills have to be paid first," he had said tersely.

Anna fought down a surge of frustration. That was when it seemed Kevin had stopped wanting her so. That was when Kevin's ardor had begun to cool. That was when it began to be weeks between their lovemaking.

She lay down on his bed and buried her face in his pillow, remembering their wedding night.

She had been ashamed that at thirty she hadn't known enough. The closer it had come to her wedding day the more she read about sex, and she had spent practically a month's salary calling Cassie who lived on the other side of the state. Cassie Zimmerman, nee Bolton, her best friend, her confidante— Cassie to whom she could say anything, but often didn't dare. Cassie, who had been fully sexually experienced by the age of fifteen and who had said she would "sample them all" before she settled down. Then Cassie had had to get married in her junior year of college. Cassie had said not to worry . . . spend a weekend with Kevin before they married. Then, she'd *know*.

But Anna hadn't wanted that. She couldn't begin her marriage that way. Her own mother had, and the arguments that Anna had overheard between her parents had been shattering, leaving Anna heavy with guilt.

That first night she and Kevin had been together had not been satisfactory for either of them and Anna had secretly wished for some of Cassie's expertise. She had learned though, Anna remembered, smiling slightly. She had been a fast learner. Sex had opened up an entire new world of emotions and images and urges. Just when she was beginning to feel confident, Kevin . . . just got . . . tired.

She wished she could manufacture an emergency so that she could call the emergency number he'd written in the back of the telephone book. He would be ordered home from Lebanon.

At the moment the telephone rang, Anna was deep in her reverie. She didn't want to come out of it. She fumbled for the receiver without lifting her head from the pillow.

"Anna?"

It was Caburn.

Her hand began to sweat; she gripped the receiver even tighter.

"I thought we were finished." Her voice was husky. There was a pause, a silence that she almost filled.

"No." Then, "I have a question and I thought you'd rather not answer it face-to-face."

She inhaled deeply. "What question?"

Another pause. She thought she heard him cover the receiver and clear his throat. "You never answered my question about Nesmith's sexual preferences."

She started to fling the telephone down, then changed her mind. "You're sick, Caburn. *Sick!*

"Don't hang up!"

It was just the impetus she needed. She slammed the receiver into its cradle.

Sexual preferences. Anna's brain raced. It sounded so sordid. Like...like blackmail. This was more than routine. Caburn knew something he wasn't telling her. There *was* something in Kevin's past. A dozen different ideas came into Anna's mind; she tried to avoid them, leaving them vague and unformed. It didn't matter. She would stand by Kevin no matter what.

The telephone shrilled again. She would tell Caburn off this time. Once and for all. She grabbed the receiver. "Stop calling me! You're obscene! Do you hear me? Ob—"

"I hear you," a woman's voice said with a trace of laughter. "You've never called me obscene before. Bohemian maybe, but not—"

Anna slumped on the bed. "Cassie! Oh. I'm sorry about...this must be telepathy. I was thinking of you only this morning."

"Sounds like you've been having a rough time of it."

For an instant Anna felt the urge to pour it all out, air everything for Cassie, get the situation into perspective. But saying it aloud would make it real, give all her doubts substance. *Give her feeling for Caburn substance.* She wasn't ready for that. She breathed a troubled sigh, forcing enthusiasm into her tone. "No, it's just the weather in D.C. It's been so unpredictable recently."

"Well, order up a few sunny days. I'm coming to Washington."

"Cassie! No...! I mean...I'd love to see you. When?"

"Can you put me up?"

Anna didn't answer immediately.

Cassie said, "Something tells me I've caught you at a bad time."

"No, not really," Anna replied, recovering her aplomb. "It's just that my mother-in-law is still here...not at this very moment, but if you don't mind the sofa? Or if Kevin's not home you can use...." She bit back her words. Cassie would have a lot to say about twin beds.

Laughter filtered over the wire. "The sofa is fine. It beats tents and cots. Wally and his dad are joining a farmers' protest against wheat sanctions to Russia—again. A holdover from that plane they shot down. But this time they're hauling tractors to D.C.

They're going to camp out around the Washington Monument, or so they tell me. I can't handle that... not anymore.''

"You used to say you could sleep anywhere," Anna teased.

"Don't remind me. I'm a staid old farm wife and mother now. Rise at dawn, bed down at dusk. I even belong to the PTA and church auxiliary.... But that doesn't mean I wouldn't like to kick up my heels a bit."

"I'm impressed." Just hearing Cassie's voice, a friend out of her past, someone she could trust, was soothing.

"Don't be." There was an odd little catch in Cassie's voice. "You know that old saying about making your bed and lying in it? Well, I'm lying in it."

"Cassie, aren't you happy? I've always thought—"

"What's happy?" Cassie shot. "I just figured out that I married the wrong brother."

Anna thought a minute. "You married Tip's father. That's not so wrong."

Cassie gave a cryptic laugh. "I married the one who'd have me. Keep it in the family I always say." She sounded bitter.

"I never realized..." Anna began and stopped.

"You're still so naive, Anna. I can hear the shock in your voice. Look, I'm sorry I dumped on you. We'll talk when I get there, okay? I don't know exactly when yet. Would you mind if I invited Wally's brother over? I need to have a few words—"

"His brother lives here?"

"In Alexandria. I've got to hang up now, or I'll catch hell over the cost of this."

"Cassie...."

"Watch those obscene callers, you hear?" She hung up.

After Cassie's call Anna wandered around the house, brooding. She liked Cassie more than anyone she had ever known, and had often envied Cassie for rushing off down paths that Anna found luring but hadn't the courage to explore. Now it appeared those paths that Anna found so appealing, those paths that Cassie had chosen, were forays into a troubled future.

As Anna passed the small table in the hall, the clock began to chime the hour. She put her hand out and touched it, as if to see if she could stop time.

ANNA HAD GROWN UP in a small neighborhood in Shawnee Mission, just south of Kansas City. Her dad, Bernie, worked across the river in Missouri in a machine shop that made plastic rims for eyeglasses. He was staid, stolid and didn't talk very much. His idea of an exciting evening was to watch television and drink beer. Anna's mother, Nadine, had been lithe, vibrant and craving excitement. When Anna started college, her mother took her aside and told Anna that she was leaving her dad before it was too late for her to enjoy anything of life.

Nadine insisted that Anna live on campus, not fall into the trap of the quiet life she herself had lived. Life was too short, she claimed. Nadine had not realized how short. A year later she became the victim of kidney failure. As she lay dying, she begged Anna to take care of Bernie. Maybe, Nadine had said, she had been wrong. Maybe God was punishing her. In her junior year of college Anna moved out of the dormitory and back home. When he was off work, her dad still sat in front of the television and drank beer. If Nadine's death affected him, he didn't show it. Now Anna wrote him once a month, letters he never answered. He refused invitations to visit.

Anna had enjoyed taking care of the house in

Mission, discovering she was miserable without someone to fuss over. It made her feel needed. That first year she and Kevin had been married had been heaven. She delighted in fixing up the house, preparing elegant little dinners for two, ironing his handkerchiefs, sewing buttons on his shirts.

Then came Clara Alice. Clara Alice had preempted those little chores.

For the past year Anna had felt only half-alive.

Snap out of this melancholia, she told herself now. *Keep busy.*

She dusted, waxed, washed and ironed, considering herself blessed that Clara Alice wasn't following behind to show her how it was done.

She thought she might be crazy, but she took a sweater out of Kevin's closet and tossed it across the sofa in the front room. She moved his shaving things from the medicine cabinet and left them on the sink.

Grocery shopping took up the entire afternoon. She bought all Kevin's favorite foods, ignoring the expense. Thick steaks, fresh asparagus, peaches for a cobbler, makings for potato salad and coleslaw, and freshly baked French bread. The disturbance in Lebanon couldn't last forever.

Her conscience was soothed, making all the thoughts she'd had about Caburn a thing of the past. She did not remind herself that it was Caburn who had put her ancient Chevrolet into running order.

When she pulled up to the curb in front of her house to unload the groceries, she saw a note flapping in the breeze on her door.

She glanced quickly around. There was no sign of Caburn. She left the motor running as she raced up the walk. The note was from Lila Hammond. She had convinced Clara Alice to accompany her to St. Simons Island. Clara Alice, the note went on in Lila's scrawl, was being just a wee bit indelicate. She didn't want Anna to know, and they had waited until they saw her leave. Only then had Clara Alice come home to pack. Not to worry, Lila wrote, she'd be in touch.

Anna expelled a troubled sigh as she crumpled the note into her pocket. It would be wonderful if Kevin was home now. Just the two of them.

She unlocked the door, threw it open and hauled the groceries into the kitchen. As she went back through the hall she heard a noise coming from her bedroom. Her mouth went dry. Then she heard a voice, muffled. She put her hand on the knob, caught herself and jerked it back. It might be Kevin. Then again it might not. It might be Caburn. But if it wasn't.... One man was talking. There might be two. She hurried back into the kitchen, closed the door and lifted the extension from the wall as quietly as she could. Listening for the dial tone, she heard instead, "Found some monthly diaries... looks like a schedule of some sort. Probably his deliveries and there's a queer-looking code...."

It was Caburn's voice.

Anna started to hang up, then held back, her curiosity rising. The other man spoke, a deep gravelly voice. "Well, bring 'em in. We'll turn them over to cryptology. And Caburn, watch yourself. Things are a little sticky up in Ellicott City." The call was disconnected.

Anna was paralyzed. Cryptology. Her heart began to thud painfully in her chest. Kevin was in serious trouble. But he couldn't be. He just couldn't be. He was loyal to the United States... just as loyal as Caburn. A swell of anger took hold. If Caburn had wanted Kevin's diaries, those flat little black books that he replaced every month, he could've just asked! He didn't have to go through her things... or Kevin's.

She hung up the telephone, hurried into the hall, thrusting the bedroom door open so hard it slammed against the wall. The mirror hanging on the door shattered into a thousand tiny shards. Caburn was at her dresser, his hands in her lingerie drawer. He might as well have been violating her. His head swung around, mild surprise flickering in his gray eyes.

"You're back sooner than I expected...."

"I just bet I am," she roared, racing across the room and slamming her drawer, catching his fingers. Her breath came in angry rasping gasps.

Caburn was frozen, and in the next instant she saw his eyes widen as the feeling in his fingers reached the nerve centers of his brain.

He moaned in shock, letting loose a string of unintelligible expletives. Very slowly he pulled open the drawer with his left hand, which had miraculously missed being caught, and withdrew his hand. He held it up, inspecting it; the skin was torn. He made a kind of strange noise.

Anna was too stunned to make any sound.

"What'd you do that for?" he asked, feeling betrayed. The pain was excruciating. He could barely get the words past his lips. Suddenly blood began to spurt from the gashes.

Anna nearly fainted, horrified. "Oh...oh...I'm sorry. No. No, I'm not. You had no right to be snooping through my things. You deserved—"

"I'll bleed to death while you're lecturing me," he said, paling visibly. "I need to sit down...." He moved to her bed, sat on its edge. "Get me some towels."

Anna jerked into motion, getting towels from the bathroom. Caburn took them from her, wrapping one around his hand.

"I didn't mean...not really..." she began.

"Get me some ice. Maybe it's not as bad as it looks—or feels," he muttered between clenched teeth. His head was swimming.

She got a bowl of ice, filled it with water, and gingerly dipped Caburn's hand into the bowl. He moaned, trying to move his fingers, which were beginning to swell. The water in the bowl was turning pink.

"I think they're broken," Caburn said.

"You're bleeding too much. You need to go to the hospital...but after that you ought to go to jail."

"You never give up, do you?" He didn't smile.

"I try not to."

"Good old loyal Anna."

The bleeding stopped finally, but two of his fingers were now misshapen. "Do you think they're broken, for sure?" Anna asked hesitantly. She was sitting on Kevin's bed, staunchly trying to keep the quavering from her voice.

He took his left hand and moved a finger on his right. They both heard the grind of bone against bone. All the blood left Caburn's face. "You want me to call an ambulance?" Anna advanced, feeling ill.

"Hell...hell..." Caburn exploded. "Where's the nearest emergency room? You can drive me."

The next several hours were a blur. Anna's senses were dulled and sluggish. She hung around the white hospital corridor, pacing, unable to keep still. When they had arrived, Caburn had made her pull his wallet from the back pocket and show his identification. The nurse whisked him immediately into a cubicle, and he had been there for over an hour now. Anna had gone to the desk so many times to ask how he was doing that she no longer objected when they called her Mrs. Caburn.

When the clerk had asked Caburn what happened, he told them he had slammed the car door on his hand as they were heading out to dinner. He had lied to cover himself—not her.

Another hour passed before he emerged from the cubicle, leaning on an orderly's arm. A doctor, brisk and businesslike, approached Anna.

"Mrs. Caburn?"

She nodded, too weary to begin protesting again.

"Your husband will be fine. We set the bones in the two fingers that were broken and stitched up the others. Now, we've given him something for pain, but he'll need this...." He handed her a prescription. "You just put him to bed, keep that hand elevated close up to his chest. If the hand begins to swell, bring him in and we'll loosen the splints."

The orderly went for a wheelchair. Caburn waved him off, took Anna's elbow, leaning heavily on her. Together they staggered out into the cold dark night.

"You don't look much better now than you did when we came here," Anna told him as she settled him in her car.

"I don't feel much better, either." The soft tenor of his voice still held a ragged edge of pain. He leaned his head back on the seat and closed his eyes.

Anna felt between a rock and a hard place. What she wanted more than anything in the world was to go home, curl up in the safety of her favorite chair...and do her worrying alone. If only she could put Francis Caburn out of her mind. *If only*. The stack of little black books loomed large in her mind. She wanted to know what Caburn knew.

She glanced once at him as she started the car. Her chin had a determined thrust as she made her decision. She didn't discuss it with Caburn as she turned the car in the direction of her own home.

He seemed not to notice or care. The medication he'd had was taking effect. He remained in the car, dozing, while she had the prescription filled; he was still groggy as she helped him into her house and onto the sofa.

As she hung Caburn's coat in the foyer closet she felt deep into his pockets for the daily diaries. They were there all right. As soon as he was sound asleep, she'd go through them herself.

ANNA SAT IN HER CHAIR, sipping tea with a novel open across her lap. She had not turned a page in an hour. Her eyes had traveled to Caburn, lying on the sofa, as often or more than they had to the pages of her book. She had gotten up numerous times to adjust the pillow beneath his blond head, touched his forehead to check for fever, probably an unnecessary act, but she couldn't keep from doing it; she realigned the coverlet where it slipped off his now unshod feet, and turned the lamp down so that the glare wouldn't burn against his lids.

An oddly happy feeling welled up in her.

She discovered she liked being in the same room with Caburn. Liked being needed by him. Guiltily, she brushed this irritating insight aside.

An hour later he began to come out from the anesthetic administered to him at the hospital. Anna was overpowered with the urge to flee but couldn't. The strange power he had over her came to life as he did, riveting her to the chair. His lids fluttered open. She watched him warily as he pulled himself up. She had propped his bandaged hand upon a pillow on his chest. As it slid away he moaned. "Keep your hand elevated," she whispered. "It won't hurt so much."

He nodded, hugging it to his chest. "What time is it?" He sounded weak.

"About nine," she answered.

"Make a phone call for me?"

She agreed, jotting down the number. "What do I say?"

"Just tell her I can't make it."

"And that you're sorry?" Her tone was frosty.

Caburn bent his eyes on her. They were clouded with more than anger. "Real sorry," he snapped, sounding stronger.

Anna had the grace to blush.

She made the call from her bedroom. The woman's name was Rose. She sounded disappointed, concerned—and sexy. Anna hated her. She gave the message briefly and hung up while the woman was still speaking.

When she returned to the living room the lights were up, shadows dispersed. Caburn was sitting up, his injured hand lying along the sofa arm. He did not ask her how the call went, or about Rose's response, for which she was thankful. He gave her a curious look as he ran his good fingers through his blond hair.

"Get me those diaries of your husband's out of my coat pocket, will you?"

Anna thought her legs wouldn't support her as she crossed the room.

"Oh, yeah," he added. "Mrs. Hammond left me a set of keys to her house for you in case of an emergency. They're in the other pocket."

Anna's heart sank. "How *did* you get into my house?" she asked, knowing the answer before he spoke.

"Your mother-in-law let me in while she was packing."

The thoughts Anna was having about Clara Alice ruled her for a few seconds. Finally she retrieved the diaries, hating herself, feeling as though it was an act of disloyalty on her part. There were nine of them, secured with a thick rubber band; Kevin had the tenth with him. They had always seemed so harmless, stacked neatly next to the handkerchiefs in his drawer. Now... she swallowed a tiny slab of fear and laid them beside Caburn on the sofa.

Her fingers unconsciously traced the pattern of a tiny red flower on the arm of her chair as she watched his face, watched him thumb awkwardly through the small books with his left hand. He looked up suddenly, his brow wrinkled in a frown.

"Want to help me with these?"

Anna was stricken. "Help you? Help put my husband in... in jail, or worse?" The dread she was feeling caused a spreading darkness behind her eyes, surging up so that she felt outside herself. "No... no... I can't. You've done what you wanted to do, haven't you? Succeeded in casting doubt on my husband's loyalty, on our marriage. He'll always be under a cloud of suspicion no matter what you find!"

Caburn's expression was filled with compassion. "Anna... Anna... I won't deny that something has triggered this investigation. I grant that you have enough sense to recognize that by now. Nothing is certain. Truly. I'm looking as much for innocence...." *For your sake,* he added silently.

"You're looking for treason!" Her words shattered the air like an exploding bullet, and then Anna couldn't believe she'd made such a stupid mistake. She watched Caburn's eyes fill with fury, his lips clamp into a thin line, the tiny scar on the side of his nose whiten.

He tossed the books into her lap one by one. "Here," he said roughly. "You look first, tell me what you see." He already knew the lie for which Nesmith was guilty. He had now to discover if that single lie had bred other lies.

Anna's heart beat heavily as she concentrated on the diaries for fifteen minutes. Each page was a compendium of flight numbers, travel times, departures, arrivals, off days. But at the top of each page, next to the printed date number was a sign, the scientific figure for male or female. She thumbed quickly, checking Kevin's off days, days she knew he had been home, days for which she was certain of his every move, his every act, every telephone conversation. She shook her head.

"I don't see anything wrong here. Just these...." She leaned forward, pointing to the signs, insisting that they could mean little, and told Caburn why. "I admit they're curious," she said hesitantly. "But they only begin in August."

"There's nothing criminal in using special reminders. Which figure has he sketched for your birthday?" The fury in his expression subsided.

"I don't know. He has the October calendar with him."

"Was he home?"

"Yes."

"Did you do anything special?"

"We went out to dinner. Clara Alice went with us." Anna's voice went flat, remembering. That Sunday when she woke, she had slipped her fingers beneath her pillow searching for her gift—Kevin had often left her little surprise gifts there. There was nothing. All day she had been happy, expectant. By the dinner hour she realized Kevin had not remembered her birthday. She mentioned it and in a guilt-fed rush he had made reservations and whisked them all out to Pier 7 on the waterfront. It wasn't the most pleasant evening she had ever spent.

"And later?"

"Later we came home, watched television for a while and went to bed."

"That's all?" His tone was suggestive, or perhaps, Anna thought, it just seemed more seductive because of the dregs of the medication.

Instinctively Caburn was watching her eyes. He saw the hurt flare in them. He wanted to take her into his arms, tell her it didn't matter, but his words seemed to jar an unhappy memory in her. He wished he could make her smile.

Anna looked away from the intensity of his gaze. "Yes," she murmured softly. "That's all." She had wanted something more that night. Kevin had gone to his bed. She, to hers. She had invited Kevin into her bed, and when he refused, almost begged him to allow her into his. Pleading with him had made her feel less a woman, and his staunch refusal had left her tense, defensive, haunted with the feeling that she was no longer attractive. Two nights later he had made love to her, quickly, hurriedly, like an afterthought, and afterward she was still filled with a hunger. That was three weeks ago. He had not touched her since.

A tiny series of sounds, a cacophony of growls made Anna look up sharply, inquiringly at Caburn.

He grinned sheepishly. "My stomach. I guess I'm hungry. I haven't eaten all day."

Her smile was faint but warm. "You're always hungry when you come here." For an instant they were almost friends.

"Seems that way, doesn't it? Put the rubber band back around those books for me, will you? I'd better get going."

A protective instinct swept over Anna. 'How are you going to drive? You have to use your right hand to shift gears. Are you going to be able to do everything for yourself left-handed?" In her concern she pictured him struggling to open doors, unbutton his shirt, unhook his belt.

"I'll figure it out, somehow. Why don't you call me a taxi, though? Driving might be more than I can handle...." He made sure his voice was carefully bland, but he dreaded getting to his feet. His body, though strong, was responding graphically to the trauma it had suffered. His weakness was exacerbated by hunger. He was looking at his injured hand, but out of the corner of his eye he saw Anna staring at him, hard. He stood up, emitting a small moan that was not at all feigned. She was out of her chair and at his side at once.

"Oh, Caburn. Keep your hand up." Her arm slid around his waist, coaxing him in the direction of the kitchen. He kept his eyes closed, gathering her nearness to him in his mind, enjoying the feel of her against him. "I haven't eaten since this morning myself," she said. "It's just as easy to cook for two as one."

She had to put a pillow on the narrow bar that served as a table in the kitchen, so that he could prop up his arm, for when he had tried to lay it in his lap as manners dictated, he had turned a sickening gray. She had to cut his steak for him, butter his bread, watch him take awkward left-handed stabs at his food and miss. He was good-natured about it. "This is worse than dunking for apples at a Halloween carnival."

She laughed. He paid her extravagant compliments until Anna was glowing. Her hair shone like a halo of brown silk around her fragile features. The haunted look left her face, making her eyes seem impossibly huge and liquid and captivating. Caburn knew he should go, but her laughter had struck a chord deep within him.

They talked for an hour, about Washington and Kansas, politics and farming, life and people and books and libraries. She learned of his mother, his stepfather, his half brother and leaving the farm to see the ocean. He had an apartment that he loved, free of clutter, and a collection of imported cloisonné boxes, painted with airy flowers outlined in gold leaf. His friends teased him about the boxes because they were impossibly delicate for so rough a man. She told him about growing up in Mission, her mother leaving and dying, and about having dinner at the Muehlebach Hotel while the New York Jets were there and seeing the lobby strewn with flowers as fans pursued Joe Namath, who hobbled through on crutches. She did not tell him about Kevin or the emptiness she often felt. It completely slipped her mind that the food he complimented had been bought for her husband.

They came close to quarreling when she suggested a pain pill. Caburn preferred whiskey.

They were playing a game. She counted Caburn harmless now that he was hurt. Harmless to herself. As their conversation wound down, the silences becoming longer at shorter intervals, Anna's mind began to thrum with questions about the investigation, questions she didn't dare raise lest she inadvertently give him information she would regret later.

While he sipped on a second whiskey she did the dishes, and as she dried and put away the last pan, Caburn said, "You can call that taxi for me now."

She had purposefully not planned past dinner. She only knew she had loved being needed. It was an emotion that had been scraping bottom of late. Her mind raced forward, picturing Caburn trying to shave, fry an egg, take a bath. Her eyes met and lingered on his a moment, and then she looked away. "You can stay in Clara Alice's room," she suggested casually.

Caburn had his answer ready. "Impossible," he said, pleasantly aggressive, his tone firm.

She turned and lifted her face to his. "No. No, it's not." He was rising to his feet, and there was a sudden urgency in her voice. "You...you can figure out what you can do for yourself...and what you can't I'll help you with. You shouldn't—"

"I don't want to impose on you more than I already have. I can get someone over to my apartment...." He let the words hang, gaining their own momentum.

Anna was thinking about the provocative voice belonging to the unseen Rose. "I won't take no for an answer," she said firmly. "After all, it's *partly* my fault that...."

Caburn took a sip of his whiskey. "Well...if you insist...."

She drew him a bath and helped him off with his shirt. Her hands trembled with excitement as her fingertips brushed his flesh. He wouldn't let her cut off the shirt-sleeve. "I'd have nothing to wear in the morning" was his excuse.

She didn't offer him one of Kevin's shirts. It seemed a disloyal thing to do under the circumstances. By the time his shirt was off and his broad solidly muscular chest revealed with its fine wiry covering of blond down, she felt like jelly. To cover her awareness of him, she bustled around with an efficiency that left no room for intimacies. But when she glimpsed his pockmarked skin, bearing numerous old scars, she involuntarily gasped. "What happened to your back?"

"Shrapnel." He shrugged, making his muscles ripple. Anna looked away. "Came too close to an exploding mine in Vietnam." Caburn smiled at her expression of horror. "It doesn't hurt."

"But it must have once," she said as she began to wrap his bandaged hand in plastic.

"A lot of things hurt us at one time, but we forget

the pain." There was suddenly an unreadable glint in his gray eyes. Anna's feeling of warm safety in his presence disappeared. "I haven't had a bath drawn for me since I was four," he said.

"I—I'll just be sweeping up that mirror," Anna replied, "if you need me for anything."

He gave her a boyish smile. "Hope you're not superstitious." His eyes were flicking over her.

Anna's heart was pounding. She backed up, a few steps toward the door. "I've saved up enough bad luck to account for a half-dozen mirrors," she told him, attempting some levity. He looked at her for an endless moment.

"Anna, I wish you could learn to trust me." His tone was soft, almost pleading, and it frightened her even more. He heard her sharp intake of breath.

"I...I'll try." Then she was gone, leaving him to struggle with his belt and pants.

In her own bedroom Anna ran the vacuum on high, just in case he did call out. When she had finished the task she had set out to do, she stepped into the hall to listen. Caburn was out of the guest bath and she could hear him puttering around in Clara Alice's room. She sighed heavily. In her own bath she twisted her silky dark hair atop her head, bathed and put on pajamas, then crept around the house as quietly as she could locking up for the night. Ten minutes later she was sprawled disconsolately on her bed.

In Clara Alice's bed Caburn was propped up on pillows, staring into the dark. His hand throbbed. He adjusted it this way and that, finally laying it across his chest. Some of the throbbing subsided. He reviewed every tidbit of information he'd come across in the Nesmith case. It was a situation in which he was damned if he did and damned if he didn't.

He felt the urge, and it was strong, to get out of his bed and join Anna in hers. He held back. Women like Anna didn't run around climbing into bed with strangers, but he was desperately aware of how much he wanted her. If only he could unleash all that emotion and anxiety she was keeping bottled up.... *If only*....

He heard her step into the hall and held his breath, heard her hesitate outside his door, and then heard soft barefoot sounds as she went back to her own bed. A twin bed. Caburn didn't wonder about the reason for that. He knew.

He listened to the old house settle, readying itself to accept the night, cataloging all the sounds, and told himself that he was going to leave first thing in the morning. No, not the first thing—after breakfast. Anna was a damned good cook. He had a niggling curiosity to know what she looked like at first light. A man could tell a lot about a woman then.

Some minutes later he drifted into a troubled sleep, the throbbing in his hand in harmony with another, a different kind of throbbing in his loins....

Afraid to dream, Anna went to sleep at once.

6

WHEN ANNA WOKE the next morning dawn had not struck. She liked to lie abed Sundays, but today she rose at once, threw on her robe, then brushed her teeth and pinned her hair loosely atop her head before she emerged into the hall. She tiptoed to Caburn's door and put her ear to it. She could hear him snoring gently. She smiled, caught herself at it, and stopped.

She should not be feeling this kind of pleasure at having a man in her house. A man who wasn't her husband. The pleasure made her feel remote from Kevin, from his little black books and from the investigation.

She found it difficult to think of Caburn now in an impersonal way. He was touching her life, whether she wanted it or not. He was delving into it, stirring it, tearing at it.

As she set coffee to perking, bacon to frying and bread to toasting, she wondered what there would be left for her to salvage when Caburn's inquiry was done. The bacon popped, spraying grease. Anna stared at it, gripped by a paralyzing moment of sudden insight. When the investigation was over, she'd never see Caburn again.

"That bacon smells good, like country cured."

She spun around. "Oh, I didn't hear you get up." His face was shadowed by his beard, his eyes dark, glowing with a passion unveiled. He wore slacks, socks and had his shirt over the crook of his arm.

"I've been trying to work my way into this but I can't quite manage."

She moved the bacon off the stove, took the shirt from him and inspected his injured hand. "I think your fingers are still swelling. How do they feel?"

His smile was touched with irony. "Like I wish they belonged to someone else."

"I'm sorry. Truly. I don't know what got into me."

"Forget it. I'll live, and it doesn't hurt as much as I'm pretending. It's just that I like having you take care of me." There was a little catch in the area of his heart. She was far more beautiful in the morning that he had anticipated. Strands of her pinned-up hair spilled down in soft wisps. She was free of cosmetics except for the elusive flowery scent she wore, and her dark fringed eyes seemed to take up her whole face.

Their eyes met and locked. Anna looked quickly away as a tiny cry of dismay escaped her lips. They had wandered onto dangerous ground. She suddenly wanted to touch Caburn, not sexually, but just to be close, to wrap herself in the warmth she could feel emanating from him. And in some far forgotten recess of her brain, she was wondering if it was possible to love two men at once. A harsh guilt stabbed at her until she tossed the thought aside, burying it so deep that it might not surface again.

Caburn reached out and touched her face, tracing the line of her jaw tenderly, gently with his fingertips. Unconsciously, Anna leaned forward, accepting his touch. "You're beautiful in the morning...I knew you would be."

"I—thank you." The courtesy rose to her lips automatically.

"Don't be afraid of me, Anna." The urge to gather her into his arms was compelling. He took his hand away, though he wanted to reach out and touch her again. He knew he couldn't. Not yet.

Color deepened in her cheeks. "I'm not," she whispered. "I'm afraid of myself." She backed away an inch, perhaps two, holding up his shirt, suddenly her old efficient self. "Let me help you with this." The quaking in her voice was almost imperceptible.

At breakfast Caburn was more dexterous at feeding himself with his left hand than he had been the evening before. They didn't engage in conversation, not even light chatter about the weather, Washington politics or the nation's economic depression. Words seemed unnecessary, and Anna was fearful of stumbling onto a subject that might grow heated. After his second cup of coffee Caburn looked up at her, his inspection now tinged with a bitterness she had not noticed earlier. He asked for a taxi and this time she complied, ordering it from the kitchen extension.

"I'll be taking Nesmith's calendars with me," he said, and she knew he was once more in the role of investigator.

"I understand." A sadness came into her huge eyes as she slipped into the breakfast nook across from him.

"Do you? Do you really understand?" He was searching her face, reaching for some clue. Anna couldn't fathom what it might be. She shrugged, her shoulders sagging, as if determination had gone out of her.

"What else can I do?" She watched a frown overtake his brow. "I'm sure Kevin will be able to straighten this all out when he comes home. Whatever it is." Her throat was suddenly dry. "You did say you were looking as much for innocence as...." She let the sentence die.

"Suppose he can't straighten it out?" He hated himself for asking the question when he saw the terror flare behind her lids. "What will you do then?"

Anna thought he spoke carelessly, but she had an inescapable premonition of doom. She put her hands into her lap, away from Caburn's prying eyes, and clasped them tightly together. "He will straighten it out. He will. He just has to, that's all."

"*But if he doesn't?*" There was nothing careless about his tone now. Anna lifted her chin, her dark brown eyes filling with shadows.

"I'll stick by him, no matter what happens." She leaned forward placatingly. "Please, can't you tell me what's going on? What prompted this? You asked me to trust you. Can't you trust me?"

Cursing himself for his lack of wisdom, his personal involvement, he stalled, reaching into his pants pocket for his pipe and tobacco pouch. "Could you fill and pack this for me? I'll tell you how."

She performed the small task with trembling fingers, helping him put fire to the tobacco, watching him inhale deeply. The cloud of smoke trailed ceilingward. "Please," she whispered. "This not knowing is so...so hard."

"I don't have the authority to say anything. My head would be on the line. I'm sorry. Look, I promise after cryptanalysis finishes with the books that I'll tell you what they found."

"Or don't find?"

"Or don't," he repeated, grim faced.

"There is something beyond those calendars, isn't there? Something that's already happened, and it's not good."

Caburn stood up, moving away from the table, away from her huge pleading eyes. He paced the tiny kitchen and felt himself filling with outrage at the unjustness in the world, at the unjust way fate dealt with women like Anna. His gray eyes went flint hard. "I'm not supposed to tell you a single solitary fact. If it will ease your mind, I can tell you that as of this minute, all we have is a civil matter. One that can and *will* be kept quiet, and be no embarrassment to either of you—outside your immediate families." He stopped pacing and stared out the kitchen window over the sink. Anna thought she actually heard him catch his breath.

"But either way," she said in a small voice, digesting his words, "Kevin will be out of a job?" He nodded without looking at her.

"He won't go to jail? You can promise me that?"

He looked at her then. "He won't go to jail, no matter what we find. I can promise you that." It was a truth that left him with a bad taste in his mouth.

An exalted feeling swept through Anna. She got up and came around the breakfast nook to stand beside him, putting her hand on his arm, brushing her lips to his cheek. "Thank you. Oh, Caburn, thank you."

Her lips were soft at the edge of his mustache, her breath warm and sweet and redolent with mint and coffee and bacon. His good arm went around her of its own volition, pressing her close, so that he could feel her breasts crushed against his chest. His indrawn breath was ragged.

A deep-seated instinct made Anna move away from him. "I'm sorry, I forgot myself."

"Forgetting could cost you," he said, his voice throttled with a controlled passion.

Anna paid no attention. It seemed the weight of the world had been lifted from her shoulders. Not knowing exactly what had caused the inquiry didn't seem so threatening now. Her future—hers and Kevin's—seemed assured. She could make her marriage work. She would, she vowed.

CABURN INSISTED ON WAITING outside for the taxi. She helped him into his overcoat, tied his shoelaces, saw him to the door, then kept going to the window every few minutes to see him standing hunched in the cold, his pipe gripped tightly between his teeth, his injured hand a slash of white as he hugged it to his chest. She wanted to go out to him, offer him coffee and conversation, wait with him. He must have sensed her at the window once because he turned to look. The expression on his gaunt unshaven face was grave, and he didn't wave.

She was pulled from the window by the shrill of the telephone. It was Lila Hammond, telling her all was well, that she and Clara Alice were settled in on St. Simons Island. Clara Alice was still being stubborn, refusing to speak with Anna, though Clara Alice did want to know if Kevin was home. Then Lila wanted to know if that nice man had still been there when Anna got home from grocery shopping. She hoped that it had been all right to leave him alone in the house. He had said he was a friend. Anna smiled into the telephone.

"Yes, it was all right," she said, though she knew that, in spite of everything, Caburn was regretting the intrusion. After she hung up she raced to the window. Caburn was gone.

As the day wore on, Anna puttered around the house, feeling lost. Only yesterday she had been enthralled at having a bit of unexpected privacy, enthralled at having her home to herself. There was something so vital about Caburn, so alive, that made the house seem empty without him.

She deliberately shut off this dangerous avenue of thought, forcing her mind to dwell on her love for Kevin, whipping up her flagging loyalty, and dedicating herself anew to the purpose of putting her marriage back on track.

She knew exactly how to begin.

ENERGY SEEMED TO FLOW into her veins. She began dismantling the twin beds in her room. From here on out, Clara Alice would have to suffer sleeping in a single bed.

Dragging headboards and footboards and slats and mattresses and springs was wearying. Anna feared her strength would give out, that she would have to spend the night on the sofa for a place to lay her head. But by late afternoon she stood on the threshold of her room, surveying her handiwork.

It was as it should be, she thought. Her bed was in its rightful place. It was a great old carved masterpiece of glistening Philippine mahogany. She had found it propped forlornly against a wall at a rummage sale. It had taken weeks to remove the layers of paint from the intricately carved leaves and flowers. And even more weeks to refurbish the wood with boiled paraffin. Now it hugged the east wall, framed between bedside tables whose lamps cast a soft incandescent glow over the thick, peach-colored comforter.

Unbidden, the image of Caburn lying in it rose up to haunt her. She pictured him naked, his arms solid, his thighs taut below a thick chest covered with blond down. She closed her eyes, banishing his image from her brain. Caburn had no place there. Not in her thoughts...not *that* way, or in her bed.

She had to keep busy.

She took a bath, shampooed her hair, blow drying it until fine strands framed her face like thick silken thread. She applied soothing astringent to her face, her eyelids, and a touch of rouge to her cheeks. She stepped into tan gaberdine slacks, topping them with a brown knit sweater that fit loosely, so that there was only a bare suggestion of the fullness of her softly rounded breasts.

In the kitchen she stuffed a roast with garlic and set it to marinating in oil on a shelf in the refrigerator. The minute Kevin called from the airport that he was on his way home, she'd pop it into the oven. Whether it was today, tomorrow or the next. Weary, but with that comfortable exhaustion that comes from a day well spent, she made herself a cup of tea, taking it and a favorite book into the front room. She listened to the national news on television.

More marines were being shipped to Lebanon. There was no news about the peace legation. For all she knew, Anna thought, Kevin could be on his way home right this minute. Rain and sleet were forecast for that night and all day Monday. A little thing like bad weather couldn't dampen her spirits now. She remembered her marriage vows: *For better or worse*.... No matter what Kevin had done, she would be with him, stand with him, lend him her courage, her strength. She wouldn't ask him *why*, regardless of what he had done.

She got up and turned the sound off, leaving the picture on. She couldn't get used to the emptiness of the house. She turned on all the lamps in the living room before she curled up in her chair once again and tried to lose herself in Agatha Christie.

ANNA LIFTED HER HEAD with a jerk, tilting it, listening. Something had awakened her. She had slept, and soundly too, if the lethargy she was feeling was anything to go by. Andy Rooney glared at her from beneath bushy brows from the television as he wrapped up his segment of ''60 Minutes.''

She couldn't recall if she'd been dreaming, yet coming awake so abruptly set her off-balance and she had a sudden premonition of disaster mounting invisibly like the silent swell of a huge wave before it innundated an unsuspecting island. Annoyed, she chided herself for the thought. Caburn had promised her Kevin would not go to jail, promised that whatever had triggered the inquiry would be kept quiet. That meant Kevin's reputation would be kept intact, that he would be given a job referral, a right to live his future even if the past had a spot of rust.

Yet deep inside she couldn't shake the strange sense of something being very wrong. She stood up, about to go into the kitchen when she paused, listening once again. Of course, the wind was picking up, rattling the eaves of the old house.

She took another step and stood rigid. There. She'd heard it again. Not the wind. A rustling near the vestibule, then a soft rap on the door. Another. Anna went limp with relief. She had overworked herself changing beds, that was all. And she was hungry. Hungry stomachs made for peculiar thoughts. She laughed at herself as she approached the door and glanced through the viewer.

A young woman stood on the steps, bundled in a thick wool car coat, a sleeping, snowsuited infant cradled in one arm, a diaper bag slung over the other. Lost, Anna thought—or having car trouble. She opened the door and peered around its edge.

"Yes...?"

"Anna Nesmith?" the young woman inquired hesitantly.

"Why...yes, I'm Anna Nesmith," she replied, taken aback at having been personally addressed by a stranger.

The girl's lovely mouth widened into a grin. "Oh, I'm so glad I found you before Kevin got home. He'd kill me if he knew I'd looked you up. I know you had a falling out over your dad's estate, but I feel so strongly about families sticking together.... And, I want to mend fences if I can." The words were rushing out with an evangelistic urgency, as though she was afraid Anna would slam the door on her.

"Mend fences? Estates?" queried Anna, thoroughly muddled. "Who are you?"

"Oh, I'm sorry. I thought I told you. I *knew* I'd get this all wrong, and I've been practicing what I'd say all the way down from Ellicott City." She laughed. "There I go again, digressing. I'm Janie, Kevin's wife." She shifted the baby on her hip. "And this is—"

Anna heard no more. She felt herself collapsing like a marionette whose strings had suddenly been cut, yet a greater force than her horror kept her standing on the threshold, kept her upright. The force did not extend to her hand and it slowly slid down the cold doorframe to grip the knob as her knuckles went as white and bloodless as her face. "Kevin's wife... ?" came out in a strangled whisper. "Is this a joke?"

A tiny frown wrinkled the girl's creamy brow. It took Anna traumatic seconds to notice she had huge violet eyes, and she was young, much younger than herself; twenty-three or perhaps twenty-four... oh, Lord! Perhaps even younger.

"I'm a surprise, I know," Janie was saying, "but I didn't even know that you existed until after our wedding. I told Kevin he should have at least called to tell you and his mother. And I begged him to invite you to the baby's christening, but he insisted the rift between all of you was too wide to go back."

Anna wanted to run, to put distance between herself and this appalling conversation, this lie she was hearing. She could feel herself going numb, could feel that silent wave washing over her, drowning her. The hand that hung limp at her side moved of its own volition, fluttering to her heart. "Do you know who *I* am?"

"Of course. You're Anna, Kevin's sister. He told me all about you. You and your mother live together. Please may I come in, even for just a moment? The wind is so cold on the baby."

The baby. Anna knew she was hanging onto her sanity by a thread, and couldn't credit her own ears when she heard herself saying, "Please do," as quietly, as pleasantly as she would have spoken to Lila Hammond. She stepped aside to let the girl enter, waved her toward the sofa, then reached a chair just as her knees buckled. Her eyes were riveted on the baby as the girl who called herself Kevin's wife lifted a blanket from the diaper bag, spread it on the sofa, laid the baby upon it and unzipped the snowsuit, revealing a tiny head covered with silken dark curls. Curls the same color as Kevin's.

She moved her attention quickly to the girl. Janie Nesmith didn't look criminal. Didn't look vicious or even like "the other woman." What Janie Nesmith looked like was: sweet innocence, charming, happy, not at all furtive, or guilty of sin, or guilty of stealing another woman's husband. Anna felt a nausea rising in her throat and swallowed it back. "How... how did you find me?" she asked, groping for something to say, something casual that wouldn't give her away.

The girl's hand stayed protectively on the baby as she looked up at Anna. "Oh, I bought Kevin a wallet for his birthday and thought I'd surprise him by exchanging it for his old one. I came across your name and address on one of those emergency cards. You know the kind I mean?"

Anna nodded. She couldn't make her brain function. She couldn't keep on listening to this girl-woman who called herself Kevin's wife. She couldn't because she'd come apart and everything inside her would fall out.

Then she was thinking: *I'll tell Kevin when he gets home and he'll take care of it. He's so good about handling things. I'll just sit here and smile, admire the baby and pretend. Then when Kevin comes home, we'll have a good laugh about it.*

The baby squirmed but didn't wake. Janie patted his backside as her wide violet eyes darted around the room then settled once more on Anna. "You have a lovely home. Everything is so wonderfully *old*. I love antiques, but Kevin won't have anything but modern."

"He won't?" Anna said dully.

"He's set in his ways. But I guess you know that." She leaned forward, her eyes appealing. "Please, I want you to know first off that I'm not here to ask you for money. I don't care about the settlement and that Kevin was left out. I tried to explain to Kevin that it was better for his dad to leave you and his mother cared for. He can take care of himself and us."

Anna wanted to scream that there was no will, no settlement. Instead, she smiled wanly and brushed a strand of hair from her face. "How . . . how long have you and Kevin—" she could barely form his name on her lips "—been married?"

"Fifteen months this Tuesday. Is Mrs. Nesmith here? I so want her to see Kevin, Jr. Maybe it will soften the way she feels about Kevin. . . ."

Anna felt a jolt, as though she'd been stabbed with a huge knife that impaled her to the chair. "Kevin, Jr.?"

"We call him Junior. Kevin adores him and I was thrilled to have a boy first. We hope for a girl next time."

The knife was twisting. Anna was hearing Kevin: *"You know we can't afford a baby, Anna. Wait."* This was all a nightmare. She would wake up any min-

ute. She heard herself saying, "Clara Alice—mother—isn't here right now. She's on vacation with a
neighbor." *But if she was, she'd have another stroke,*
Anna thought. Her fingers gripped the arms of the
chair. "After you found my name and address,
Kevin told you about me?"

Janie gave her a wry little smile. "Not at first, but I
can be such a nag at times. He told me I was never to
contact you. I...even if you don't want to see Kevin,
I hope we can become friends. I thought with the
baby and all...well, little Kevin should know his
aunt and grandmother. It's not fair to him.... Oh,
I'm rattling on again.

"I'm nervous, I guess," she continued, leaning
forward, a tiny frown forming on her brow again.
Anna caught a slight tremor in the girl's voice now.
"I—I've come...I confess I've come for more than
one reason. I—I think Kevin may be in some sort of
trouble. There's been a security man from the State
Department where Kevin works at our house, asking questions. Have they been here? I'm so worried
and now they've shipped him off with that legation
to Lebanon, and...."

Anna didn't know whether to laugh or scream,
but the scream was taking over, building from deep
inside her, building...building, until it was a roaring in her head. She closed her eyes. She was having
a dream, a bad one, but she was coming awake, she
could feel it, and the scream was silent. When she
opened her eyes she would be alone. There wouldn't
be this innocent-looking woman sitting across from
her. There wouldn't be a baby with Kevin's hair lying on the sofa. She would be alone...alone...
alone. From far away she heard a soft gasp.

"Anna. Anna! Are you all right? You've gone so
white. I know my coming here like this has been a
shock. I should have called first. Oh, please. Are you

angry? I'll go. I'm so sorry. I've done the wrong thing."

Anna wanted to open her eyes, wanted to say something soothing to the young woman; tell her how pretty the baby was, tell her that she was mistaken, that Kevin was her own husband. Each time she came close to reaching the light that was bursting behind her eyes, the darkness swooped down upon her, suffocating her, forcing her eyes to stay closed as if leaden weights had been attached to her lids.

She heard those small rustlings again. The wind in the eaves. A voice coming from somewhere.

"I'll just leave my phone number and address here on this bench. We live in Ellicott City.... Please, after you've thought about it, will you call me?" A soft sweet voice, pleading, a baby gurgling happily, a gust of cold air, a latch snapping into place...silence, and the earth slid away.

7

CABURN WAS WEARING tweed slacks and a black cash-
mere sweater that contrasted starkly with the white
of the bandages on his hand. He felt like a fool always having to have his right hand tucked up
around his throat, but the throbbing pain was
damned bad whenever he dropped the hand to his
side. It had taken him thirty minutes to shave left-
handed this morning, and he was nicked like an
adolescent on his first try. So much for safety razors,
he thought irritably. He slumped lower into the old
leather chair and glared at Phipps through slitted
eyes.

"This doesn't add up to a hill of beans," Phipps
was saying. "There's no Swiss bank account, we
can't find where Nesmith has had any contact with
foreign elements—or with any friendlies on our
own turf, either, as far as that goes. All we've got
here is a jerk with two wives, a stack of monthly
travel diaries with a code that cryptanalysis is shaking their heads over, yet *somewhere, somehow* Nesmith has come up with an eight-thousand-dollar
chunk of money to put down on a cottage in Ellicott
City."

Caburn came alert. "Eight thousand dollars? Anna
said she gave Nesmith eight thousand dollars for the
down payment on their house in D.C. two years
ago."

Phipps rummaged in the file before him. It had
grown thicker over the past week. "The sneaky bas-

tard. He bought the D.C. place with a VA loan, a dollar down. He must've stashed it away. That'd explain it, but where'd she get it?''

''Saved it, working as an assistant librarian at the University of Kansas.''

''Easily checked,'' Phipps said, making a' note. ''Now, ain't that going to be a kick in the teeth when she finds out?''

''I'd hate to have to be the one who tells her.''

Phipps frowned. ''Yeah, well, don't think you're going to get to duck this one. The word from upstairs is no publicity. They don't want the press poking their long noses around here. Too many delicate negotiations going on right now. If push comes to shove, we'll sweeten the pot if we have to.'' He grunted and fell silent, seemingly absorbed in packing his pipe.

Caburn watched with dismay. No way he could pack his own left-handed. He'd taken up cigarettes to curb his craving for nicotine. He shook one out of a pack and lit it up. He wanted to leave. They'd covered all the new information on the case, discussed Nesmith's diaries at length, and planned strategy for the coming week at which time they hoped to wrap things up. The Nesmith women's lives would be in shambles, but that wasn't State's worry. But every time he thought of Anna there was a humming in his head. He remained sitting, shifting his solid weight on the old leather. He had the feeling Al Phipps had something else on his mind. It was the first time in their long association that silence between them made Caburn squirm.

He watched Phipps test the draw on his pipe, watched the smoke curl upward, and watched Phipps's watery eyes settle on his own.

''You say she just came over and tapped that drawer?'' Phipps's expression was solemn.

Caburn winced. He should've known. "It might have been more than a tap."

Phipps studied his pipe as if it was a new toy. "How much did you say this Nesmith woman weighed?"

"A hundred ten... fifteen, tops."

The old man thought about that for a minute. "What she done to you don't hold a candle to what Louise done to me." He was grinning.

Caburn stood up and exited from the office, dragging his raincoat behind him.

Phipps hung his great ugly head out the door as Caburn was stabbing angrily at the elevator call. "You got to learn to take this with good grace, Francis!"

Caburn could hear his boss braying with laughter. He regretted every snide sly remark that had passed through his mind and that he'd held back when Louise had shot Phipps. The old dog.

Alone in the sanctum of the elevator, Caburn allowed himself a tiny grin.

ANNA CAME AWAKE in the chair, gasping for air. She'd been having a nightmare. The room was dark. Not the dark of night, just filled with gray and an odd arrangement of shadows. She couldn't recall having turned out the lights. The sun had risen on a new day, but its sharp golden light was hidden behind black scudding clouds.

She felt bruised, as if she'd fought a battle and lost. Achingly she dragged her body from the chair and then it all came back to her, the knowledge like a vaguely remembered dream. She walked slowly around the house, touching things like a blind woman might, putting things into their rightful place in her mind.

It could be a lie, but she knew it wasn't. She was

thinking off and on about Caburn and the inquiry.
There was no mystery about that now. The department had stumbled upon Janie.

She thought of those huge innocent violet eyes.
She wanted to hate the girl, the mother of Kevin's
son. She wanted to call her vile names and couldn't.
They remained only formless ripples in her mind. It
came to her that Janie was a victim, too, and that for
the baby, the tiny infant with Kevin's hair, it would
be far worse. But she couldn't expend sympathy on
them. She was the one suffering. . . .

Kevin had betrayed her. Not his country. Betrayed
her whole existence. Infidelity. Such a simple easy
word to pronounce, yet it wrecked her, mocked her
and was the specter of failure.

She made up excuses for Kevin, searching for the
single reason he had done this to her, the only possible answer coming like a crushing blow. He didn't
love her; he never had. She was ugly; she was old.
And she couldn't forgive him for giving Janie what
he denied her.

She could feel the pain surging up, filling her, enveloping her like a mist rolling in on the Potomac.
She couldn't seem to move away from it, escape it. It
followed her into the kitchen where she made coffee,
which she couldn't drink. It followed her into the
bathroom where she brushed her teeth and gagged.
It followed her into the bedroom where she stared at
the bed. And then it began to swallow her whole.

Her bed. His bed. Their bed. The hours spent in
lovemaking drifted into her mind, but there had
been other hours, too. Long frustrating nights spent
alone . . . no, not alone. Clara Alice had been here.
Anna gritted her teeth. While . . . while . . . .

She saw Kevin making love to her, saw her legs
wrapped around his lean slender frame and then the

legs weren't hers, but another woman's, a younger woman's....

Her brain shrieked at the picture, refuting it, trying to erase it, but it wouldn't be erased; it hung there like a living thing, writhing, a horror, vile, defacing her life. A new gargantuan wave of pain swelled within her and with it came an inferno of rage, a violent unsheathing of frustration and anger. Oh, she knew what Kevin had done to her now. Kept her as custodian of his mother while he took himself off to another woman's arms where ne could get out from under Clara Alice's talons. Clara Alice will have to be told. *And Clara Alice will blame it all on me. I blame it all on me.*

She snatched off her clothes and went to inspect herself in the mirror behind the bedroom door. But the mirror was gone, shattered, as her life was shattered. She didn't have the strength to pick up the pieces. Emotional pieces. She stood there for a moment, dumbfounded, then drew on a robe. Tears were beginning to slide down her cheeks and great choking sobs thrust up from her throat.

The telephone shrilled; she let it ring, an insistent accompaniment to the rage that was a torment now. Her hand reached out to the instrument of sound. She yanked it from the wall. She was doing something! It felt so good. The torment demanded attention, surfeit. She snatched up the covers on her bed, their bed, and tossed them aside, swirling them around her head until they billowed and sank to the floor. She knocked over lamps, turned over the chaise longue, she dragged all of Kevin's clothes out of his closet and stalked outside in the sleet and scattered them around the tiny yard. Sweaters and ties clung to bushes like bizarre decorations. She tossed his shoes, left foot, right foot, onto the roof. She was wet, shivering, but didn't feel the cold; she couldn't seem to stop. She talked to herself, she screamed her rage, and finally when his closet was bare, she went back into the house and fell across her bed to die.

As Caburn paid the cabbie he glanced at cars parked along the curb, finding his own several lengths from Anna's. He couldn't drive yet, but he was getting the hang of being one-handed now. He kept everything he needed in his left-hand pockets: cigarettes, lighter, loose change, wallet.

He watched the taxi move off into the gloom and hunkered down into his coat while his hat shed water down his collar. He turned to face Anna's house, stopped in his tracks and stared, disbelieving. The tiny yard was cluttered with clothing—pants, shirts, sweaters, an overcoat—a pair of undershorts was being carried down the sidewalk in a gushing rivulet of rain. His foot touched something soft—balled-up socks.

The back of his neck prickled.

He hurried up the sidewalk, taking the steps two at a time, knocked on the door, waiting impatiently, tried the knob and found the door unlocked. He slipped into the vestibule. Wind and rain gusted past him; a piece of paper fluttered to the floor from the small narrow bench. He bent to retrieve it, an automatic gesture, scanning it briefly in the dim light. An unintelligible noise broke from his throat and a quiet grimness tightened his face.

He heard a sound that made him go deathly still. A keening ululating sound, made more eerie by the gloom and silence of the house. He had heard such stark strange wailing in Africa and Vietnam when he had come across women mourning their dead. His mouth went dry but he made his feet move.

She was huddled on a sheet half-torn from the

mattress, curled into a fetal position, and the keening low moans were guttural, resembling those of an animal who has crawled off in the forest to die.

"Anna..." he whispered to her, calling softly, crooning as he switched on the light and made his way across the room, stumbling over the debris, kicking what he could out of his way. He ran his hand over her quickly, expertly, finding her unhurt physically. He took a breath and sighed.

He talked to her; silly things, he thought, but he kept talking. "You're going to be all right. I'm going to take care of you. Don't worry...." She kept her eyes closed and her whimpering continued. He found blankets and covered her. He found the telephone, cursing when he discovered it had been yanked from the wall.

He went into the kitchen and, using the telephone extension there, called Phipps. "All hell's broken loose at Nesmith's," he said when his boss came on the line. "Ellicott City's been here." There was a dangling pause and he could hear Phipps strumming his fingers on the metal desk.

"Stay with it. See what you can do. Get her calm at any cost. What about the old woman? How's she holding up?"

"Not here, gone on vacation," Caburn said.

"Goody for us," said Phipps with stolid sarcasm. "Do you need any help?"

"It wouldn't hurt to send someone over to clear up the front yard. She's tossed Nesmith's clothes out and they're floating down the gutters."

Phipps sighed. "She would've done that sooner or later anyway. Find out if she's called anybody. Now, I'd better see what's happening in Ellicott City. The last thing we need is a bunch of hysterical women on our hands."

After he hung up, Caburn shrugged out of his

coat, tossed his hat on the kitchen table and, as rapidly as he could, readied a pot of coffee. When he thought he'd need it, he set it to perking.

Anna stirred as he reemerged into her room. She raised herself up on an elbow and blinked, trying to get him into focus. "Caburn, is that you?" Her ashen face showed no surprise and when she spoke her voice was cool, as if she was past emotion.

"I'm here," he answered, going around the room, righting tables, lamps and the chaise longue as best he could. He worked his way to her side.

"Why'd he do it? Kevin, I mean," she asked, her voice small. "He had a good job. He had me. We *did* love each other. *We did.*" Her eyes followed him as he prowled the room. "Do you know what he did that hurts the most? He let her have a baby... *a baby.*" Her voice caught in her throat. "But not me. Noooo, not me and I've been trying so hard to get pregnant. I'm ugly. He must've thought I'd give birth to a monster."

Caburn picked up a pillow, placing it behind her head, then sat down next to her on the bed. "You're not ugly," he said gently, brushing a tangled mass of hair wet with rain and tears from her face. "You're beautiful. Vulnerable, loyal and beautiful."

Her hand grasped his wrist. "Then make love to me. Make me *feel* beautiful. Make me be a whole woman again. Please," she whispered when she saw his face going hard. "Please, Caburn, make love to me." Her eyes blazed, lit with an edge of madness. He read the anger, the hurt, the confusion in her expression. "There's something going on between us," she continued in that same raspy tone. "I can feel it. I know you do, too. I've seen the way you look at me." Her voice took on more intensity, her eyes dark and bottomless, veiled by her lashes. "Do you know what our little Janie thinks? She thinks I'm

Kevin's sister. She—" Longing washed over her with a force she could neither stop nor resist. She put her hand on Caburn's arm. "Just make me whole again, please...."

Caburn realized her whole body was trembling, trembling more than he was. He felt a searing beginning in his gut, a kind of wildness that he'd never before experienced; a dry forest ignited; a fire storm roaring, enveloping all in its path, and he thought for an instant he might be consumed. "You just need some rest. I'll sit here with you. When you feel like talking, I'll listen, and later I'll make coffee or we can go out for a bite to eat."

"Eat?" She laughed, a sound fractured with incredulity and hysteria. "I don't want to eat. Food sustains life. I don't have a life. I'm nothing. I *have* nothing." He turned slightly away from her, from the desperate quality in her voice. If he touched her now....

He's rejecting me, too, Anna thought. She couldn't let him. She leaned against his back, running her hands over his shoulders, feeling his thick muscular arms. There was no fat, no softness anywhere. She felt him shudder at her touch, felt him responding. "Oh, Caburn," she whispered throatily. "Do you find me ugly? Am I useless...?" She brushed the back of his neck with her lips.

"Anna...Anna," he uttered hoarsely. "Don't touch me like that." He twisted to face her, his hand rising to grasp her shoulder, his fingers biting into her flesh. "You don't know what you're asking. I want to kiss you. I want more than a kiss. I want everything you're offering. I want you naked and I want to crawl all over you, touching you like you've never been touched, lov—" The vein in his temple throbbed and pulsed with emotion. "But I don't want you like this. Not in a thousand years like this. Later you'll hate yourself... you'll hate me." He could still feel the lingering sensation of her lips on his nape, and he tried to curb the heat that was growing savagely in his loins. He was aching for her now to the point of agony.

She jerked free of his grasp, kneeling in the middle of the bed, her eyes suddenly alight with an idea. "You knew all the time, didn't you? Even before you came here that first time? You've known all along that there was another wife... a baby...." She choked back a sob.

"I wish it could have been different," he said tenderly. "I never expected—I'm sorry."

"Oh, God!" she exclaimed in a hoarse whisper. "Caburn. *Sorry?* I don't want your pity. *I want to be loved!* I want to know I'm a woman. Don't you understand? Don't you see? It'll be my sin, not yours—and you're not pure, you've had other women. That Rose you had me call—you've been to bed with her, haven't you?"

His brows lifted, watching her. It was furrowed and threaded with pain. "No. Besides, other women are different."

"Different?" There was a clear rising hysteria in her voice now. She spread her hands, beseeching him. "How? How am I different from them? Look—" She clutched at her robe, threw it off and knelt before him on the bed, naked. "Look at me, Caburn. Don't close your eyes! How am I different? Am I too old? Too wrinkled?" The need in her was mounting, the hunger to assure herself that she existed, that she was alluring, desirable. "Don't you think I can please you?" Her voice fell. "I need you." She dropped her face into her hands, her hair, silky and catching the light, fell forward, brushing her creamy shoulders.

Caburn swallowed. There was no turning away from her now. He could see the ridges her ribs made in her flesh as she breathed in and out; he could see the softness of her belly from navel to...his mouth went dry and his heart was beating with palpable intensity and he could feel himself losing control. He couldn't keep from touching her and so reached out to cup her chin in his hand, raising her face to his. He could barely speak. "Anna...."

She didn't think about what was happening or what she was doing. She gazed at him, searching his expression, his eyes, finding acceptance, salvation, concern. For now, it was enough. She'd make it enough. She lifted his injured hand to her lips, trailing kisses over the bandages, pressing her mouth hungrily to his fingertips exposed at the end of the splints. "I'm sorry that I hurt you," she murmured. "If I had known...."

There is a threshold of endurance, whether it's the threshold of pain or pleasure, and Caburn knew he had stepped across it. His arms went around Anna, crushing her to him, and he buried his face in her hair. She smelled of rain and tears and flowers. He took a deep heaving breath and sighed.

"I know I'm not," Anna said, her voice muffled against his chest, "but tell me I'm beautiful, Caburn. Tell me I'm loved.... Make me *believe*." While she was talking her hands moved along his chest, unbuttoning his shirt, unhooking his belt. "Turn off the lights," she implored softly. "Please. I don't want you looking at me now. I don't want...."

Caburn summoned his will and found it wanting. "You're going to regret this, Anna." He went across the room to switch off the light and made his way back to the bed in the dark. He let her finish undressing him.

"Will you regret it? That's all I want to know," she replied in a hushed whisper as he cradled her in his arm.

Her flesh was soft, lovely, like silk beneath his hand, and warm.

"Never," he answered, and gave up a throaty moan as her hand fluttered gently over his face, his eyelids, his nose, his chin, his lips. When she pressed her lips to the throbbing pulse in his muscular neck his arm tightened around her.

He fed his hunger at her mouth, at her breasts, devouring her, finding surfeit time and again.

Anna vented her pain on his body, searching every inch as though looking for that opening into which she could crawl for refuge. She fondled, caressed, finding pleasure, warmth, ecstasy. She molded herself to the unyielding contours of this thick strong frame, looking for safe harbor, and she felt the force of his raw and savage virility stirred to wondrous heights, and welcomed it. She abandoned her despair, her anger, her hate. She lost herself in a world gone soft and porous and did all the things she needed to do. She loved, she cherished. Beneath Caburn her body arched and sang, answering a music, a beat, a drum only she could hear. It was the music of ancient pagan rites, of womanhood, of fertility.

Caburn loved her, succumbed to her charms, tortured by the knowledge that the pain he was comforting was on behalf of someone else.

AT DAWN THEY LAY SILENT and very close together, not talking, just listening to one another breathe. Anna had her head on Caburn's chest. He felt her lashes, feathery, catching on a hair that grew around his nipple. It was one of the most erotic sensations he had ever experienced. He wondered if her eyes were open, if she could see his growing need in the dim and shadowy light.

After a moment she stirred, moving her head to

his shoulder. "Are you awake?" Her tone was hesitant, cautious. Caburn felt a stab of apprehension coiling in his belly. She wanted to talk now; he had dreaded this moment, knowing it was coming for hours. "I'm awake," he answered.

"How old are you, Caburn?"

It wasn't a question he'd been expecting. He smiled his relief into the dark. "Thirty-eight, going on my next life."

Her head came up abruptly; a strand of hair caught on his mustache and he blew it gently off his lips. Anna looked at him though his profile was only a vague shape in the dark. "I was that bad?"

"You were that good." He turned on his side, propping his injured hand on her rounded hip. "Anna," he began and stopped, thinking, then tried again. "I don't even want to say his name here in this room, have him between us. But I feel he's here. His presence. Whatever reason we find, if we find one, for Nesmith's double marriage, it's not going to be you. It's not going to have anything to do with sex." He pressed his mouth to her forehead. "I want you once for me, just me," he told her.

The silence between them lasted several heartbeats. "Remember the time when you told me that you almost married? What stopped you?" She whispered the words even as she shifted closer, until the tips of her nipples and thighs were touching him.

"That's not something I like to talk about, especially now."

"But you know everything about me, Caburn. I want to know about you."

He sighed heavily. "In a sentence?"

Her fingertips were rippling over him again; exquisite, gentle touches on his neck, his shoulders, his arm. "That's not fair. You never let me get away

with just a sentence. Why didn't you get married?
Did you love her?"

"I thought I did. She preferred my half brother."

Anna caught the bitterness in his voice. Oh, she
knew just exactly how he must feel. She said quietly,
"Why do you suppose God makes us suffer so?"

It wasn't a question he felt equipped to answer.

Anna knew that she had not begun to think deeply about her situation or about the decisions she was
going to have to make. She had not yet come to
terms with her husband's infidelity. Making love
with Caburn had restored some of her equilibrium,
neutralized some of the hurt, and when the cathartic
effect wore off, she knew she'd be plunged into depression. She wanted to push that time as far into
the future as she could. She pressed her lithesome
body against Caburn's. "I guess you've changed
your opinion of me," she remarked throatily.

"What opinion is that?" His breath was coming in
shallow gasps.

"That I won't respond to a man's carnal desires...."

His mustache brushed her cheek as his lips sought
hers. "Hours ago," he whispered, and his hungry
lips closed possessively over hers. And as the earth
revolved on its axis at a speed of more than a thousand miles an hour, Anna let go a world she thought
had flung her away.

SLEET BEAT AGAINST the kitchen window and in the
ruffled light above the sink, Anna's dark hair had a
golden cast. It was swept atop her head, revealing
the regal column of her neck and how well it set
upon her shoulders. The décolletage of the caftan
hinted at symmetrical upthrusting breasts, then
flowed over her rounded hips to whisper at her
ankles. Sitting at the breakfast nook, his eyes tracking her every move, Caburn was enthralled, still

feeling the length of her flesh, warm and passionate, against his own.

The tension in the air between them was acute. Anna was acting embarrassed. He could tell from the way she was sneaking looks at him when she thought he wasn't looking, that what they had done was beginning to take shape in her mind. He had hoped, expected for them to have some sort of grace period, a few hours, before Anna sank into melancholia. Her depression had begun while he was showering. He had stepped from the bath with his blond hair awry and a towel draped around his hips to find her stuffing his socks into a bag along with more of Nesmith's. "Hold it," he had called. "Those are my socks."

She had turned on him with a strange little smile. Not happy, not sad, more like she was surprised to find him there still. "It's funny, isn't it? How all men look the same from the ankle down?"

An odd feeling had come over him and had stayed with him. He had never seen Anna smile...a genuine, happy, letting-go smile that lifted to her luminous dark eyes. And then he thought: When he waltzed into people's lives, they usually didn't.

Now she was setting bacon to sizzling and cracking eggs into a bowl for omelets. She was thinking aloud, and every now and then he put in a comment to keep her talking, hoping it was therapeutic.

"I'll have to tell Clara Alice when she gets home, and I don't know how or where to begin."

"Let that be for a while. It might be best coming from an official source."

Anna kept her profile to Caburn. She couldn't make herself look at him. "She'll blame me for all of this; I know she will."

Caburn sipped his coffee. "As long as you don't blame yourself."

Her hands became very still, poised above the frying pan. "I have to be at fault. I must be. There has to be something missing from me, or else why didn't I have Kevin's love? Marriage vows are sacred...oh, I wish I was dead."

"Anna!" Her words electrified Caburn. He knew self-hatred bred self-destruction. He'd seen it too often. Especially in war, where men were required to do the vilest acts; they hated themselves for it, and the next time took chances no sane man would. A death wish. He fought the urge to snatch Anna up and take her into the bedroom and love some sense into her. This passive acceptance of hers was dangerous. He had to get her angry, get her mad and get her fighting. He had to push her to the point of risk. "Now I know why you don't want my pity," he said scathingly. "You want to flagellate yourself, become a martyr."

She spun around, her eyes finally making contact with his. "That's not true! My feelings are hurt. My heart is broken, my life destroyed...."

"You're all grown up; you ought to know that some men won't be bound by monogamy. You just picked the wrong guy to marry and then put the blinders on."

"I didn't!" Her protest was vehement. "There was no clue.... He came home from work when he was supposed to.... He—"

"He worked a hell of a lot, didn't he? Was gone a lot of weekends and holidays? You didn't ask a hell of a lot of questions, did you? You made it easy for him."

She turned back to the stove. "I don't believe in nagging. I watched my mother nag my daddy right up until the day she divorced him. A year later she was dead. Nagging makes for divorce and I don't believe in divorce."

"So your mother nagged. Could be she saw she'd married a loser."

"My dad's not a loser," she said stiffly. "He's just set in his ways."

"And after your mother left, you moved back home and took care of him. That says a lot. He let you do it. You bought the groceries, did the cooking, did the washing. That left him free of any responsibility for himself, didn't it? What does he do now? Sit in front of the television?"

Anna's mouth tightened. Caburn was homing in on a truth she didn't want to see. She drained the bacon of grease, poured frothy eggs into the pan. "I don't want to discuss my parents. That's not the issue here."

"I'm just trying to point out that the pattern was set. You were easy pickings."

"I fell in love. That's something you wouldn't know anything about." She slid the half-cooked omelet onto a plate and shoved it across the sliver of a table toward Caburn. He glanced at it with a snort of disgust, got up, moved around her and put the raw mess back into the frying pan.

"Sit down and drink your coffee. I can manage this one-handed."

"Good for you. Superman to the rescue."

He ignored the sarcasm. "There's something else you may have to face."

"The worst has already happened," she remarked, daring him to dispute it. She gave a little shudder as she sat down, collecting herself in an instant. She needed desperately to speak of herself, of her life with Kevin, if only to give some immediacy to her past, make it all seem worthwhile. But that kind of relief would also be an ordeal, a gnashing of mind and teeth, and inevitably she would be returned to the present. This present, where divorce loomed like a dull thud. "I don't want to hear any more."

"Well, you are going to," he said adamantly, as he slid the now-cooked eggs onto his plate and returned to the table. "Nesmith left a paper trail. A clever one, because he's had us going in circles. What made it jell was that he listed Janie's address on his hospitalization policy, so when she had the baby the records showed an address in Ellicott City, but he requested that the check for the hospital bill be sent here to Fountain. Later he insisted on picking up the check himself. It takes a lot of juggling to support three households all at once; his mother's, yours and Janie's, and it takes a nice slice of change, too. Nesmith owns the house in Mission, by the way, not Clara Alice, and she can't go back there because it's being rented out."

"You're lying."

He shook his head. "Since Janie got pregnant, Nesmith's been consolidating his resources like any good businessman."

Anna was beginning to believe and see. Her eyes flickered, smoldering now with outrage. "You're making me sick. I've been turning my paycheck over to Kevin every month. *Every single month.* Are you telling me that I've been helping him support his other wife?"

"And his mother, don't forget." He set his fork aside, took up his cup, looking at her over its rim. "You know he gets a retirement check from the army, don't you?" Anna nodded, but she hadn't known. "We're checking every base where Nesmith was stationed. You might be wife number one, then again you might not."

Anna's heart began to pound and race like a jackhammer. "No... no. Please stop. Oh, what's going to happen to me?"

Caburn wanted to tell her that she'd never be rid of him, but now wasn't the time. For all his practicality, for all his harshness, he was a romantic. Anna needed routine to get her through this...ordinary everyday routine—going to work, coming home. And above all, she needed to be independent. All the confusion she was feeling was readable across her wide expressive brow. "It looks to me like you're just going to have to take care of yourself," he told her.

"I want to talk to my husband," she said suddenly. "I want to hear his voice. *I want him home.* You can send for him."

Caburn froze, recovering almost at once. "Does he usually call you when he's on assignment like this?"

"No. But I want *him* to tell me that he doesn't want me. I want him to tell me to my face. I don't want to hear it secondhand from you. You've slept with me now, haven't you? So you have a vested interest. If I kick Kevin out that leaves me available for you."

His eyes narrowed to slits, but the fury was there in his face, in the way his mustache twitched and in the harsh line of his mouth. "You're being very selective in your recall, Anna Nesmith," he said silkily. "Let's keep the personal element out of this. And the next time you try luring me into your bed, I won't come. How's that?"

Anna had the grace to blush.

"Let me point out something to you. You may be the spurned wife, but so far the law is on your side. That little Janie, and she's a nice young woman, and her baby, are the victims. She's a schoolteacher on leave of absence for her baby's first year. A scandal like this is really going to hurt. She's the other woman. Everyone's sympathy is going to lie with you. I expected you to have some compassion. You don't. I wish we'd had this conversation before I stepped into your bedroom." He rose to his feet, stalked to the telephone and called Phipps to send him a driver.

"You're cruel," Anna told him when he hung up. "The cruelest man I know."

His laughter was harsh. "That's saying a lot, because you're married to a real dud. His clothes are all in plastic bags out by the curb, if you're wanting to haul them all back inside. And if Janie gets in touch with you again, keep up the pretense that you're Nesmith's sister. That's an order."

"That's not fair!"

"There's more at stake here than being fair. I'm going to the doctor to get the stitches out of these fingers. I'll be back later. I'll expect you to have called the library and given them some acceptable excuse why you haven't been to work in two days."

Anna's anger was all-encompassing. "An excuse? I'll just mention that I've been playing musical beds with the State Department."

His grin was tinged with irony. "The problem with you, Anna, is that you can't accept the fact that you're a woman with needs, like any other woman. It's not something you bottle up and store like perfume, you know. You haven't yet come to terms with your sexuality. You seem to think sexuality is a by-product of marriage. Tell your supervisor anything you want, but you're going to need that job." His tone was filled with ominous import so that Anna realized he was still keeping information from her. He turned to leave, then stopped, eyeing her with a glance that went from head to toe. "Another thing—you make a lousy omelet."

"Get out of my house!" she screamed. "Get out of my house and get out of my life!"

"Sure. Until this afternoon." He grabbed up his

coat and sauntered toward the vestibule, knowing Anna was hard on his heels. "There's no going back, Anna," he tossed over his shoulder. "You know it. You can fight it, but going to bed with me made that final. Put it out of your mind...if you can."

But she couldn't. After he left, the house reeked with Caburn's presence. He was in the kitchen with her when she washed the dishes; his mesmeric quality engulfed her as she put the bedroom in order. She went hot and cold at every reminder of his touch; putting fresh linens on the bed made her body surge with sensual recall—the way his hands searched her body; the way his lips scoured her; the way every part of him that was man devoured her, thrust into her. Above all she remembered how wantonly forward she had been, so that for an hour after he had gone her face was flushed and radiant.

She didn't want to admit the truth of his parting words. She could never again be a wife to Kevin Nesmith. That part of her life was now an island with an insurmountable moat. She had burned the bridge that looked to her past, and foundered on the path of the future. She told herself that she must endure, that she must survive.

In all the months she had worked at the library she had never taken an unscheduled day off. She had sick leave built up. She was sick, and sounded so when she called to ask for the remainder of the week off. It wasn't every day a woman found herself to be a member of her husband's harem.

She spent the afternoon going through her picture album.

There she was on her first day of school. Lanky, her knees knobby. She found a pressed corsage... her first prom, and she couldn't remember the name of the boy in the picture with her, which had been taken in front of the mantel by her mother. There was the first picture of herself with Kevin, taken on a picnic. They had asked a passing teenager to snap it. She was looking at him adoringly; he was staring straight into the camera.

Their wedding day. In the chapel at the university. Her father in a suit and tie, looking uncomfortable. Cassie, standing next to him, grinning, with her hand on her son, Tip's, shoulder. Tip had the expression of boredom only a nine-year-old can muster. And herself, radiant, looking at Kevin. He was staring straight into the camera's eye.

Anna paused and tried to remember when Kevin had stopped looking *her* in the eye.

She was in the kitchen pouring tea when she heard Caburn's return. He pounded on the door, not so hard at first, but growing impatient, then insistent. Let him stand out there in the drizzle, she told herself. She wouldn't let him in ... ever. He'd have to knock the door down.

After five minutes of pounding, with the thudding reverberating throughout the house, her resolve slipped, and every step toward the front door was a step toward fury.

8

"CASSIE!" ANNA'S MOUTH GAPED as she stood surprised and transfixed before her friend.

"I've banged on this door until my knuckles are raw! Have you gone deaf since you came to Washington?" Cassie Zimmerman was wet, bedraggled and exasperated. Her huge eyes seemed to be looking at Anna from behind their sockets, but her spirit was as abrupt, gay and sharp as always. "Do I get asked in out of the rain...or not?" she said, dropping her bag and hugging Anna to her thin chest.

Anna regained a measure of her composure and laughed. "Yes, you get asked in. I thought you were someone else." She extricated herself from Cassie's arms and picked up the suitcase. It was soaking wet and she hurried Cassie into the spare room to unpack it, raising questions as she went from case to closet. "Why didn't you call me? How did you get here? Where are Tip and Wally?"

"I got here by taking the train and sitting up a day and a night—the easy part was a cab from the station. I didn't call because I wanted to surprise you. I didn't expect you to be home from work this early. I thought I'd have to tackle dear old Clara Alice."

"Well, you surprised me," Anna said, watching as Cassie towel dried her short blond tresses. "And Clara Alice is on an impromptu vacation with a neighbor."

"A wonderful respite for you," said Cassie with heartfelt sympathy. "So, where's the master of the house? Am I interrupting anything?'' She gave Anna a telling smirk.

"Don't be crude. Kevin's in Lebanon with a peace legation, so we have the house to ourselves." Of all the people Anna knew, Cassie was the sole person with whom she felt she could talk about her problems, yet an uncharacteristic caution made her hold her tongue and pass the opening her friend had inadvertently provided. "Where are Tip and Wally?" she repeated instead.

"Driving cross-country in a semi, hauling their tractor behind like male Bo Peeps. They joined up a caravan in Missouri. All farmers coming to Washington for the protest. Wally promised to call when they get here and send Tip over. Against his wishes, of course. To eleven-year-olds, mothers are a bore...."

"That's one label he can't stick you with," Anna said, smiling.

"Hah! The gossip that titillates elders doesn't appeal to kids. Believe me. To Tip, I'm old, as in O-L-D." She ran her fingers through her hair and fluffed it out. "I'll do, I suppose. Now, if you will just lead me to the fireplace before which I can languish away with a cup of tea, or, if you have it, something stronger?"

"Sorry. No fireplace. But tea, bourbon, brandy or white wine I can provide."

"Start with hot tea, then a small glass of bourbon with a tiny sliver of ice, then a glass of wine and a piece of cheese.... Oh, Anna, remember those days when we could survive on anything?" Cassie said wistfully.

"I remember when we thought we were invincible," Anna said, taking Cassie's arm and leading her into the kitchen.

"I LOVE THE WAY you've done up this old house," Cassie said admiringly. "You always were so domestically clever. I envy you that."

They had had tea in the kitchen, but now were ensconced in the living room, Anna in her favorite chair, Cassie curled up on the sofa with her feet tucked beneath her. Both were sipping on bourbon and the sliver of ice had long since melted.

"I'm glad you're here," Anna said hesitantly. "I've needed a lift."

"Well, puff up and tell me all about it," encouraged Cassie. "I'm interested."

Anna waved her hand dismissingly. "No, you first. What was that you were telling me on the telephone about Wally's brother?"

Cassie's expression went grave. She inhaled deeply. "If I had to do my hairy youth over again, I'd be more circumspect. I'd be like you, with nothing to regret."

"We all have regrets," Anna put in softly. She should know, she thought with silent introspection. But she didn't want to think of her situation. Better Cassie's, whose problems were always so solvable.

"Not like mine, I'll warrant," her friend was saying. "You said it yourself. We thought we were invincible. Well, I thought that invincibility lasted a lifetime. Now I know it doesn't."

"So, you just grew up, Cassie. We all do. You just took longer than most of us."

"Where was all this sage advice when I needed it?" snapped Cassie. She was immediately contrite. "I know. I wasn't listening." Her green eyes took on a faraway look. "I liked to party, I liked sex...I wanted it all. Remember? I said I'd pick the best of the bunch and get married. Then I got stupid or careless or both, and I got pregnant with Tip. If I'd just stopped fooling around...but no! I had to have one last fling. I've never told you this, but I think Tip's father is Wally's brother." She cut a glance at Anna. "You don't look shocked."

Anna shook her head sadly. "Nothing shocks me

anymore, Cassie. Go on with your story...." She suffered for a moment beneath a skeptical glance from her friend. "Well, some things may shock me, but nothing you do does. I'm used to your streak of wildness. It's this matronly air I can't get over."

Cassie raised her glass. "Touché," she said with a weak grin.

Anna laughed. "Are we getting drunk?"

"Possibly. Now, where was I? Oh, yes. I had set my cap for Wally's older brother. Half brother actually. But Wally always seemed to be trying to outdo his brother, and after he and I had...had bedded down, to say it nicely, good ol' Wally had to go boasting to his brother. Back then, I didn't think it mattered who fathered babies...they were the flowers of love. Now I know better."

"You've been married to Wally for almost twelve years now, so why is all this so important all of a sudden? Wally accepts Tip as his son, doesn't he?"

"Yes, and I wouldn't tell him any different."

"You did say you kept it in the family—"

"That's just it. The poor side. Frank is the one who actually owns the farm and I think Tip ought to inherit."

"Why don't you just ask Frank to make Tip his heir? Or does he have a family of his own?"

"No, he's not even married. And I *have* put it to him—every summer when he gets home for harvest. He refuses. He said he wouldn't give away his heritage to the result of a questionable liaison. Can you imagine that? A questionable liaison!"

Anna frowned. "Doesn't he like Tip?"

"Oh, sure. Adores him, in fact. They get along splendidly. But I don't think Tip should be penalized for my actions. It's not fair. That's another reason I wanted to stay with you while I'm here. I want to get in touch with Frank. He wouldn't be caught dead going near a protest march. His government job, you know—he has to keep up appearances."

"Answer me this, Cassie. What makes you so sure *Wally* isn't Tip's father?"

"Well, I went to bed with Frank first, and you know what they say. It only takes once...."

"Not necessarily," Anna suggested with a logic she knew by heart.

Cassie dismissed this negative with an airy wave of her hand. She closed her eyes for a moment, resting her head on the back of the sofa. "Can you believe this is me talking? I, who would never be hampered by convention, now want my eleven-year-old to inherit a piece of this fine old green earth."

"But why is this so important now?" Anna repeated.

"Because I don't want my son to be a slave on that farm. He loves it; I don't think he'll ever leave it. He ought to own it."

It was a judgment for which Anna had no response; what thoughts she did have she knew Cassie would give no weight. For several seconds she was at a loss for words and looked down at her hands as if they could conjure answers out of thin air. She spoke hesitantly. "I guess sometimes the world seems all out of balance, doesn't it?" Again she felt the urge to pour out her heart, but Cassie thought her a misguided perfectionist. Anna was afraid of censure, and censure was the one thing she couldn't abide from her friend.

Cassie lifted her head and her eyes pierced Anna. "So tell me...what's the snag here with you?"

"Snag?" asked Anna, caught off guard. She should've remembered Cassie's ability to change subjects at the speed of light.

The other woman gave her slow grin, revealing

fine small teeth. "What snag? C'mon, Anna," she coaxed. "We were raised on the same block. You never skipped a class at school or cut classes in college. If you agreed to baby-sit and were later asked to a slumber party, you baby-sat—you gave your word. Now I arrive in Washington and find you home in the middle of a workday. You've never missed a day's work in your life, excluding your mother's funeral. And I don't ever remember you being sick. So something's up."

Anna scrambled for an acceptable reply, one not exactly a lie. "It may sound odd, but this is the first time in more than a year that I've had my home to myself. I'm not as gregarious as you are, and with Clara Alice gone for the week...it just seemed too good an opportunity to pass." She was thankful that she had switched beds, and then Caburn loomed large in her mind, and she faltered. "Anyway, I have a good bit of sick leave and vacation built up, so I'm taking some of it."

"There's nothing wrong between you and Kevin?" Skepticism took up a large part of Cassie's tone.

Anna was saved from having to form another white lie by a loud and rapid tattoo on the front door. She froze in her chair, knowing who it must be this time.

"Well, aren't you going to answer it?" Cassie prodded.

At that moment Anna thought that the entire fabric of her life had been woven carelessly, loosely, while the threads dangled and came unraveled at all the wrong moments. "No," she said firmly. "No, I'm not. I know who it is, and I don't want to see him." A pink flush tinted her porcelain skin at the intense curious expression she received from Cassie. "It's— it's not what you're thinking," she stammered quickly.

"Who said I was thinking anything?" Cassie told her. "Except I'm wondering why you won't answer that door. Whoever it is, is going to knock it down. Do you want me to answer it? Tell him you're not available?"

"Would you?" breathed Anna, relief flooding through her.

"Sure. It's no skin off my nose." She rose to her feet, brushing wrinkles from her skirt. "But," she said, "after I've gotten rid of him, you'll have to promise to fill me in."

"I'll think of something," Anna said, forcing a smile.

"You never were good at jokes," Cassie sniffed and sashayed to the door.

Anna tilted her head, listening hard, trying to hear every word spoken, but Cassie's voice was muffled. Caburn's was grainy, unmistakable, harsh, and she thought she caught a trace of surprise in his tone. Of course, there would be. He had been expecting *her* to answer the door. In the next instant she knew Cassie had not been successful in keeping him out because he was barreling across the room toward her.

She rose to her feet to meet him head-on and noted absently that he had a fresh bandage on his hand. The expression on his face was alien to her and she had seen a wealth of them cross his face. She looked beyond him to Cassie, who was white lipped with outrage.

"Sorry, Anna," hissed Cassie. "I couldn't keep him out." There was a subtle emphasis, a knowledge in her words—as if knowing Caburn, one couldn't.

"You have no right to burst in here like this," Anna said, her eyes darting from Cassie back to Caburn. "Get out."

Caburn wasn't listening, he was flailing his injured hand toward Cassie. "How do you know her?"

Now Anna recognized that alien expression. Linked to Caburn's voice was astonishment. "Cassie is my best friend. She's not any of your business. I told you—"

"I think—" put in Cassie, sidling up to Anna with a funny little smile on her lips "—that everybody here knows everybody else. Let me introduce you formally to my brother-in-law. This is Frank, the government busybody I was telling you about. Small world, ain't it?" she finished with a cynicism bordering on contempt.

Caburn stood quietly, measuring the situation, watching Anna fill with anguish as unbelief swept through her.

Anna was certain she couldn't be hearing what she was hearing. She looked around her wildly. There was no denial from Caburn. Stupified, she said, "No, his name's Francis—"

"Only to his mother," Cassie said archly. "You couldn't count the broken noses he's left behind in Cheyenne County."

"This is some sort of sick joke," Anna said, feeling an ache that was making her curl inside. She spoke as though Caburn had evaporated. "Cassie? He's the Frank you were telling me about? The Frank who's—"

"The one and the same," Cassie interjected, her contempt becoming stronger. "Nice specimen of a man, don't you think? All those thick muscles and that lovely blond hair. But don't sidetrack me, Anna. What's he doing *here*?"

Anna bent her head, closing her eyes, seeing Caburn making love to Cassie in her mind's eye. Seeing Kevin making love to Janie. She told herself she should never have married, told herself that she should never have come East, told herself that she should never have gone to bed with Caburn. Oh, all the things she shouldn't have done and had were haunting her now. She made a tiny sound in her throat.

Caburn, whose eyes had never left Anna, came to life. "Cassie, get me a glass of brandy, whiskey—anything!" he ordered, and Cassie moved into the kitchen. His good arm went around Anna. "Sit down before you fall down."

"Don't touch me." She shook him off. "Don't you ever touch me again. You're no better than Kevin."

His eyes narrowed to slits. "What's Cassie been telling you?"

"The truth. Like Janie told me the truth. I've been so stupid. So dumb." She sank back in the chair purposefully, remaining militant.

"You have every right to be bitter," said Caburn, speaking softly and moving a few inches away. "I want you to stop thinking of me as anything but an investigator right now. Let's take this one step at a time."

"One step?" Her eyebrow rose. "Are we playing 'May I?'?"

"Anna, I don't like the sound of your voice. You've got to keep your wits about you."

"Sure I do. Wouldn't you, especially if you had just discovered yourself to be one of a string of no telling how many wives? Of course I'll keep my wits about me. Didn't I go to bed with the man who's doing all the muckraking? Wasn't that smart of me?" Her voice broke and a sob began working its way from a knot in her chest.

"I'll never regret it, so stop trying to make it

sound dirty. It wasn't and it isn't. Now, shake out of this. There are things that you're going to have to do—''

"What things? What things? You think that you can command me just like you have Cassie?"

"Like Cassie, what?" her friend said, coming into the room bearing a snifter of brandy and handing it to Caburn. He gave it to Anna, wrapping her trembling fingers around the glass, holding his own over her until he was certain of her grasp.

"Nothing," Caburn replied to Cassie, as he moved away from Anna and began shrugging out of his coat.

"What are you doing here, really, Frank?" she asked, gazing at his bandaged hand with utter curiosity.

"Working." He gave her a look that would have cowed anyone less insulated behind their arrogance than Cassie. "And you can't stay here. I'll get you a room at a hotel."

"No! No, you won't," Anna said defiantly. "She's come to see me and she'll stay here until she's ready to leave. I like her. I don't like you."

Cassie smiled. "Didn't you hear Anna say we were best friends?"

"You're your own best friend, Cassie. Anna just hasn't discovered that yet. I don't want you here."

Anna's fury overrode her sense of betrayal and bitterness. "You cannot come in here and dictate to me or my friends. I won't tolerate it."

Caburn dragged up a chair and sat down, running his hand through his wiry short curls. "All right," he said wearily. "The damage is done now. We'll work it out later."

"You're not making any sense to me," Anna said. "And there's not going to be any 'later.' I'm selling this house. I've just decided. I'm going back to Kansas City. That's where I belong."

"Like hell. You're not going anywhere," Caburn snapped. "I'll put a man on this house and place you under house arrest as a conspirator if I have to."

"Isn't he wonderful?" Cassie slung with bald audacity. "So manly and macho."

He turned on her. "You keep your mouth and your snide remarks to yourself, Cassie. You can snip at me all you want when I'm home, but I'm on a job now and you will not interfere. Don't push your luck with me. It's already stretched thin. Where's dad and Wally?"

"Driving cross-country in a protest caravan, hauling their tractors," she answered. She wasn't mellow, but she was no longer abrasive.

"And Tip? Did he stay with mom?"

"No. He's with Wally. I came on a few days ahead so I could get in some girl talk with Anna. We haven't seen one another since her wedding." Cassie stood up with a smile for Anna. "My head's spinning—from the wine, not this enlightening conversation. I think I'll take a nap before dinner." She stretched luxuriously. "We *are* having dinner?"

"I'll take you both, my treat," Caburn said.

"I don't want to go anywhere with—" Anna began.

"Sure we do," insisted Cassie. "Haven't you noticed how charming and pleasant my brother-in-law is? Besides, he's loaded." She smiled now at Caburn. "Choose someplace nice, Frank, dear. And expensive. I'm in the mood to party."

"You always were," he muttered.

"You've never complained before," she said and glided from the room.

"I can see that you and Cassie are good friends,"

Anna said when her friend had disappeared into the hall. There was a snippet of jealousy in her tone and she wished she could call it back. "Other men's wives are really a speciality with you, aren't they?"

"She wasn't anyone's wife when I knew her, as you're suggesting I knew her." He began to stalk the living room, a habit he had acquired over the years. The faster his mind worked, the faster he paced. He crossed to the windows, standing there a moment in reflection, then came back to the sofa to gaze at Anna. For a long while neither spoke.

Anna lifted her eyes from the brandy glass she held in her lap and tracked him as he moved impatiently around the room. "Cassie's the woman you almost married, isn't she?"

Caburn didn't like the direction Anna's inward or outward probing was taking, but trying to shade the truth now would be disastrous later—and there *would* be a later. "Yes, she is," he replied, observing Anna, watching her reaction. She was looking straight through him, as though he was invisible.

"And Tip is your son?" she asked faintly.

"No."

"You think no, but you can't be sure."

"That's between Cassie and myself. But, you're correct," he said formally. "I can't be sure. Neither can Cassie. She was promiscuous by her own admission. Tip could be mine, he could be Wally's—he could be anybody's. That year Cassie came West, she was having a high old time. I'm not faulting her, I'm just not going to give my name or heritage to a child that I'm not certain is mine."

"You could have tests—"

"Sure. And in the process destroy my brother. And my mother. There's no doubt in Wally's mind that he's Tip's father. It's too late to stir up this sort of trouble in my family. I won't have it. Cassie knows it. You know, you're beginning to sound like an irate relative who wants me to do the right thing by Tip. I already have, insofar as possible, without making an issue of it."

Anna went silent, keeping so still that for a long while Caburn thought she had dropped off to sleep. The old clock in the hall struck the hour. Anna pressed her fingertips to her forehead. "I'm going crazy," she said into the air.

Caburn cursed under his breath. He had a few days, a week at the most, to put this investigation to bed. He couldn't allow the delicate timetable that Phipps had worked out to be upset. "You've had to absorb a lot in just a few days. But if you think you are, you're not. You're still in control."

"No, I'm not. I'm just outside me, watching. I feel like two people. It wasn't really *me* who met Janie and the baby. It wasn't really *me*—" her voice dropped an octave "—who went to bed with you." The brandy seemed to have loosened her tongue and her thoughts, her unrest. Her eyes were burning, her insides felt warm as she remembered Caburn slipping his palms under her breasts, taking their weight gently. She let out a breath that was an inadvertent sigh.

Caburn felt his heart sinking. Anna was rambling, carrying the conversation in several different directions at once. From experience he knew the brain has a wonderfully repressive mechanism—incidents, crisis, pain, which we cannot face or handle, get lost in the subconscious, allowing one to function. He thought Anna was precariously close to this state. It took him a second to do a mental about-face. He opened his mouth to speak and stopped. Better to let her talk it out.

"It just hurts so bad that I've been betrayed. I can't believe I was so stupid to fall in love with Kevin. I should've known something was amiss. I had to! It bothered me that so little of Kevin seemed to be around the house—a man ought to cause some disarray."

Caburn's mustache twitched. "I'm a slob. A real slob around the house. Socks everywhere, tobacco and ashes in everything. Dishes piled in the sink, newspapers in the bathroom." The last remark just slipped out and his cheeks flared a bit red.

If Anna heard him, she gave no indication. She paused in her own mental exercise, looking up at him, her eyes wide and unblinking. "Do you know why people fall in love?"

"I've been asking myself that question now for days," he murmured.

"What?"

"I said, a look, maybe. Chemistry. The color of one's eyes. I don't think anyone really knows. It just happens."

Anna gave a short bitter laugh. "Yes, it does, doesn't it? Lover beware...." Her full provocative lips tightened. "You know I don't want him here when he comes home." She was finding it difficult now to say Kevin's name aloud, and *my husband* stuck in her throat. "I don't ever want to see him again."

"If that's what you want, you won't have to." Her sweater was low-cut and he could see ivory shadows in its décolletage. He forced his eyes up to her face. "Why don't you take a nap, like Cassie? I'll make reservations for us at a new place I know. Very quiet and good food."

"You think food is the answer to everything." Her voice was toneless as she handed him the snifter. Escape to her bedroom was all that was left to her. The reality of her situation was sinking in. Her life would never be the same. Caburn watched her leave the room, then drank the remainder of the brandy like a man gone thirsty and looking for succor.

THE PROSPECT of going out to dinner with Caburn and Cassie was appalling, but Anna went anyway. Cassie was her guest and wanted to go, so she felt obligated; besides, she couldn't offer an acceptable excuse unless she told Cassie everything. Now she couldn't. Not after knowing about Cassie's and Caburn's old liaison. But deep inside she did believe Caburn when he said Cassie was of the past, and he had a right to his own past. Everyone did. Anna felt that fate had betrayed her. Kevin had betrayed her. And she couldn't keep from feeling that Caburn had, too. That left only God, and he wasn't listening to her.

Anna was trying to be gay and failing miserably. Little had been said among them for fifteen minutes. The thought of being entirely alone terrified her and kept creeping into her mind. The thought of having to be the one to tell Clara Alice about what Kevin had done, that he was a bigamist, that he had another wife and a child, was terrifying, too. Suppose the telling of it caused Clara Alice to have another stroke? She'd let Kevin tell her himself. That's what she'd do. Then Clara Alice could go live with Janie and Kevin and their baby. And then, she, Anna would be alone. Very alone. She didn't know how she could cope. She had never been truly alone in her life. She shrugged dispiritedly as she gazed around the restaurant.

Caburn had chosen Duke Zeibert's new place, and the old restaurateur was a walking Washington Monument himself. Newspaper and magazine articles and pictures of Duke with presidents, sports figures and astronauts lined one wall, and the elegant old man, always a presence, had greeted Caburn effusively. Cassie had been impressed, but was now making unhappy noises. She thought the restaurant far too quiet. Cassie wanted some excitement.

Anna's troubled eyes strayed to Cassie's fingertips, resting lightly on Caburn's arm. This was a new Cassie she was seeing. A coy, flirting, pouting Cassie. Or, Anna thought wryly, maybe it was the old Cassie and she just hadn't been paying any attention. Like she hadn't been paying attention to what Kevin had been up to. She sipped on her Rémy Martin, furious at herself for her own weakness. It reminded her sharply of her father. He did the same things over and over again. Even when her mother had left him, even after her mother had died. He continued to move through his narrow-walled existence as though nothing had happened. She never wanted to be that way. Perhaps, Anna mused, burying one's head in the sand was a genetic flaw.

She lifted her eyes, meeting Caburn's glance. Protectiveness was mirrored in his eyes, and kindness, perhaps something more. But she couldn't accept it. If she had been worthy of love, Kevin would have loved her. There was an endless pause as their eyes held. Caburn moved his arm from beneath Cassie's fingertips and reached out to touch Anna. "You're not eating."

"I can't. I'm sorry."

"I understand." His tone was quiet, with that authority she had noticed that first night. That first night. She didn't want to remember how easily she had succumbed to his powerful essence. It made her feel ashamed. Put her on the same level as Kevin. She wanted to ask if he could understand that, too, but she didn't. She took up her fork and stirred the food on her plate. She had taken a taste. It was wonderful, but she knew she couldn't swallow.

Caburn was being only as polite to Cassie as good

manners and family ties dictated. He had eyes only for Anna. She looked so fragile. Her dark luminous eyes were haunting beneath the preoccupied expression that kept her lovely brow furrowed in a tiny frown. She wore a one-piece, black silk dress with an oriental collar that circled her slender neck and gave an added elegance to the simple silken chignon into which she had fashioned her hair. Very small loops of gold were attached to her earlobes. He felt the urge to lean over and loosen her hair, let it cascade down her neck to her shoulders. He bent near her, inhaling her fragrance, speaking for her ears only. "I've told you before...stop worrying. You're going to come out of this all right."

"I just wish you would tell me what you know. I have this feeling you're holding something back."

The tenderness he had been displaying changed into that grimness, that hard warrior exterior that had made her ask had he ever killed anyone when she had opened the door to him a week earlier. "I don't want to keep things from you, Anna. There is more. You'll know as soon as I can tell you."

Cassie stirred and excused herself to the powder room.

For a fraction of a second Anna closed her eyes. "The wife is always the last one to know, right?" She spoke with a vehemence. "My life is coming apart at the seams and you say everything is going to come out all right. I feel like I'm on the edge of a precipice and I'm about to lose my footing. If you think that's all right...." She felt the tears beginning to well up behind her lids and stopped, fighting them, ordering them away with no success.

Caburn watched her eyes widen, saw a tear escape and slide down her ivory cheek. He brushed it away gently. "Let yourself cry if you want to. Don't try to be so damn brave." The way he said the words was like an endearment. His brow clouded for an instant. "This trying to save face in front of Cassie isn't going to work. Wouldn't you rather she go to a hotel?"

Anna really wanted to say yes. "Her husband and Tip will be here in a couple of days. She'll leave then, I guess."

"You called the library and you're going back to work tomorrow?"

"No. I mean, yes, I called, but I'm taking the rest of the week off. I—I had sick leave. I don't think I could work. I feel so leaden."

"You can't just sit around in that house brooding. If you insist that Cassie stay, then go out with her. Go shopping, see something of Washington. Go over to Old Town, browse through the shops in the old Torpedo Factory, have lunch at the Fishmarket. Keep your mind off...." His voice dropped. "I wish you'd trust me."

"My experience with men tells me I shouldn't."

"Don't judge the lot of us by one or two. When this is all over, I'll still be here."

She looked up at him, her eyes huge and sad and glistening. "I'll need friends then, won't I?"

He wanted to say he hoped she'd just need him. The smile he gave her was almost winning. "Think of this. You'll be free of an overbearing demanding unreasonable mother-in-law."

"You're talking like the divorce is already final."

There was a strange expression on his face. "Yes. I suppose I am." He glanced over her shoulder. "Well, here's Cassie and not looking any too happy, either."

"This is the deadest place I've ever been to," complained Cassie as she reclaimed her seat. "Don't they have dancing anywhere in Washington?"

Caburn sighed and sipped his brandy. "Yes, but we're not going."

"You're no fun." She cut a glance at Anna. "Just how long have you two known each other, anyway?"

"A few days, a week," Caburn injected.

Anna was thinking, *A lifetime.*

"Well, the way you're keeping your heads together anybody'd think there's something going on between you."

"There is," Caburn snapped. "An investigation. I told you. Anna is involved through no fault of her own. And don't try to pry it out of her. I mean that, Cassie, or I'll have you put on a plane for Kansas so fast you'll think you've been picked up by a tornado."

"Ah, a Washington power broker," Cassie sniffed, but there wasn't much punch in her words. She was slightly drunk. "Just don't forget, Frank, this is my first time in Washington and I want to see everything." She turned her wide blue eyes on Anna, imploring. "You can't know how stifling it is out on that farm. Nothing but old ladies and children to talk to, day in and day out. All they ever talk about is crops, weather, God and recipes...." She was becoming almost maudlin.

Caburn signaled the maître d' for their check. "Anna was just telling me she's taking you to Old Town tomorrow. It's a quaint old portion of Alexandria. You'll like that." He deflected a surprised look from Anna, but the prospect of a shopping expedition mollified Cassie, so Anna said nothing.

They waited downstairs in the lobby of the building, out of the cold, for the valet to bring Caburn's car. "Do you want me to drive?" Anna eyed Caburn's hand. He had managed to drive into downtown Washington, but she had noticed him wince with pain when he'd shifted gears.

"I can manage."

She refused the front seat, settling herself into the back, listening only halfheartedly to Cassie nipping at him. She didn't think she would ever get used to hearing him called Frank. Then, sadly, she thought she probably would never have to. He wouldn't find a place in her life after all was said and done. No doubt it was his job to keep her calm, keep her from stirring up scandal. Her thoughts turned toward hiring an attorney, filing for divorce, living alone. All the way home her world was filled with the demon, *what if?*

CASSIE WAS DONE IN FROM liquor and traveling and went straight to bed. Anna turned to Caburn. "Would you like coffee? I'll make a fresh pot."

"No. I have an early-morning meeting. Try to get some rest yourself—take something if you have it." His eyes mirrored his concern for her. "I'll call you tomorrow. Do take Cassie to Alexandria. It'll do you good." He bent slowly toward her because he couldn't help it, wanting to kiss her, wanting to take her into his arms, wanting to erase all the suffering from her face.

She took a backward step. "You'll let me know when he's coming home...back to the States, I mean."

Caburn suddenly felt desperate. But there was nothing he could do, or worse—undo. "I'll let you know," he said bleakly. He left her standing in the middle of the living room.

Anna felt an abysmal kind of emptiness as she latched the door. She had a terrible feeling of being alone. She wondered if there were other women in the world who shared her problem, shared her frustration, shared her fear of the future. She knew if there were, they must be hurting, aching and as desperately frightened as she.

9

"I CAN'T WALK ANOTHER INCH. Carry me!" Cassie was laughing, happy, her old gypsy kind of self. They stood on the cobblestones looking out over the Potomac River, watching the cold wind kicking up fluttering ripples of gray foam.

"I suggested walking shoes," Anna chastised. "Let's find that restaurant Caburn suggested, then let's head for home. I'm really worn out."

They trudged along in silence a few moments. Cassie glanced at her now and again, opening her mouth to speak then stopping as if she wanted to ask something she had no right to. Suddenly their old camaraderie vanished; Anna felt the tension rising between them as they rounded the corner of South Union and found the fishmarket Caburn had recommended. Cassie ordered a beer and it seemed to fill her with a blunt courage. "I wish you'd tell me what's bothering you, Anna. I won't breathe a word to Frank. I promise."

Anna shook her head. "It's nothing." She couldn't trust Cassie now. She was becoming suspicious of everyone, even her closest friend. Too, Cassie was drinking more than Anna could remember. Whiskey loosened tongues. For the first time in years Anna longed for her mother, for a closeness they had never had, for someone to talk with, to cry with. She wondered if the girl, Janie, had someone; a mother, a good friend. But then, Janie's life wouldn't be destroyed. She'd have Kevin.

Kevin.... Somewhere deep inside her, Anna hoped Kevin could explain away his actions. Explain away Janie and their baby. She knew it was hopeless. She felt hate and rage. She had saved her money all those years of working and living at home so that she could bring something to a marriage, have a good start. She had been conservative afterward, too, asking little for herself, hoarding and stretching her household money for special treats for Kevin, while he had been...had been.... She refused a drink. Just one and the throbbing in her throat would escape, she might become as maudlin as Cassie had last night, might find herself drowned in self-pity. She knew she couldn't let that happen. She must survive. Somehow. And alone.

Dusk was hard on them when Anna wearily pulled her old Chevrolet up to the curb in front of her home. The draperies were pulled back; the lights were on, blazing, inviting. Anna felt panic surge up and wash over her. If Kevin was home she didn't know what she could say...would say. She didn't want to face him. He probably didn't even know his bigamy had been discovered. She hadn't thought to ask Caburn. Her fingers gripped the steering wheel until they were white and bloodless.

"Good grief! Anna, what's wrong? You look as if you've seen a ghost!"

"We didn't leave the lights on in the house, did we, Cassie?"

She looked then at the house. "No, but isn't that your mother-in-law looking out the window?"

Anna glanced quickly to Lila Hammond's. The lights were on there, too. Then she spotted Lila's little blue sedan parked down the block and sighed. "Clara Alice is home sooner than I expected."

Cassie put a restraining hand on Anna's arm. "You know she and I didn't get on too well at your wedding, Anna. She doesn't like me. I hate to desert you, but I think I'm going to get me a hotel room. Do you mind? We can still have dinner together tomorrow night. . . . You won't be angry with me, will you?"

She gave Cassie a weak smile. "No, of course not. It'll probably be better that way. I'm glad we had today, anyway. I had fun."

Cassie wrinkled her nose. "I can remember times when we did have fun. Today you were just marking time." Suddenly she reached over and hugged Anna. "I know something's happening that you can't or won't tell me. And, if it includes Frank, forget what I said about him . . . and me."

"I wish it was as simple as that, Cassie," Anna whispered. "Thank you for the thought, anyway."

Cassie sighed and gathered up her purchases. "Well, if you need a friend to talk to, I'll listen, okay? Uh oh, it looks like your own personal dragon lady is getting anxious."

Clara Alice was now standing on the stoop.

"Who've you put in my room and where's my bed?" she said by way of greeting the moment Anna was on the sidewalk.

Anna closed her eyes as she bit back the retort on her tongue. "You're home early. Did you have a good time on St. Simons?" She gave her mother-in-law a peck on the cheek. "You remember Cassie Zimmerman? She was at my wedding."

"Don't try to mollify me." Clara Alice nodded disdainfully at Cassie. "You'll just have to get your things out of my room, young lady."

Anna found herself close to the breaking point. She spun on Clara Alice. "This is *my* home. Cassie is *my* friend. Please don't talk to her that way."

"I'm gone a few days and you get haughty all of a sudden. This is my son's home, too, and he promised I'd always have a home with him."

"And you will," Anna replied. There was a strangeness in her tone that made her mother-in-law take a closer look. There was a kind of tenseness in Anna she hadn't noticed before. Anna turned away from her probing gaze. "While you pack, Cassie, I'll make us something hot to drink. I think I can recommend a small hotel within walking distance of the Capitol and the Mall where demonstrators usually gather. If that will be fine?"

"Wonderful," Cassie said, rolling her eyes in a gesture that asked how Anna could abide Clara Alice. Anna pretended not to see.

"What about my bed?" Clara Alice was following hard on Anna's heels into the tiny kitchen.

"It was never your bed, Clara. I wanted it back, so I moved it." Not that it had done her much good. Only now a principle was involved and Anna meant to stick to her guns.

"Kevin won't like it."

Anna looked at her. "Kevin doesn't have anything to say about it." The tone of Anna's voice warned Clara Alice off, and a flicker of fear glazed her old eyes for an instant, but she had had her way in the household too long to give up so easily.

"We'll see about that when he comes home."

"I think," Anna said, measuring her words with care, "that we'll see quite a lot when Kevin comes back to the States."

Two hours later Cassie had reservations at the Quality Inn on 16th Street, across from the Australian Embassy, which pleased her greatly. After she left, Anna puttered around the house, feeling lost. Clara Alice had retired to her room and to the twin beds, showing her disfavor by slamming doors and drawers.

Lila Hammond called with profuse apologies about the early homecoming and, with much sympathy in her voice for Anna, said, "Clara Alice is a chronic complainer. I forgot—" she added with a short burst of laughter "—that the walrus Ace and I tangled with didn't talk." Anna told her thank you, the respite she'd had from her mother-in-law had been heaven-sent. She dreaded to think what would have happened had Clara Alice been home during Janie Nesmith's unexpected visit. And a tiny corner of her brain and all of her body relived those stolen moments with Caburn every time she closed her eyes. It made some of the emptiness go away.

She had just crawled into bed when he called. She reached for the telephone, then realized only the extension was working. She hurried into the kitchen. There was some impatience in his voice. "I was beginning to think you hadn't got home yet. Did you have a nice day?"

"Clara Alice is back." She heard his intake of breath.

"Say nothing to her, Anna. Do you think you can manage a few more days? I have to go abroad. I'll be back on Saturday."

"Abroad?" A strangled whimper broke from her as she leaned against the wall for support. "Are you bringing Kevin home?"

He hesitated for an eternity. "Yes, I am."

"What's going to happen?" She could barely speak.

He was evasive. "I'll be with you every step of the way, Anna. I'm on your side. Don't forget that."

"No one's on my side."

Caburn sighed heavily. "You can't just stop trusting people. Do you want me to move your mother-in-law out while I'm gone? Or send someone over from State to stay with you?"

She declined and gave him a message from Cassie. There seemed to be nothing more to say, but she clung to the telephone as though it was her lifeline to a sane world. She kept clinging even after Caburn hung up.

She couldn't abide being home with Clara Alice. Every moment reminded her of Kevin and his betrayal. She went back to work the following day. No one teased her about a miraculous recovery because she looked so ill. She had lost weight; there were dark circles under her eyes that made them look huge, and there was a sadness etched in them that hadn't been there before.

Cassie called her at work and was thrilled with her hotel. The Bleeker's Café and Bar off the lobby was an "in" place and there were all those lovely Australians to visit with. Caburn had been in touch with her late the night before. He had heard from Wally and his stepdad. They would be in Washington that night. Anna declined a dinner invitation to join them, though she would've liked to have seen Tip. It was a waste of money for anyone to buy her food. She couldn't eat. She was existing on hot tea and an occasional slice of buttered toast.

On Friday, Washington papers were full of angry farmers who couldn't keep from grinning into news cameras, and tractors plowing down the Mall, but the president had decamped for California and there had been bomb threats to the White House. The demonstration fizzled. Cassie called to say goodbye. "Back to religion and recipes," she said with a burst of laughter. She volunteered the break from the farm and each other had done her relationship with Wally a world of good. "And you know what? Tip just went crazy over the whales at the Smithsonian. He says he wants to become a marine biologist!"

"Then he's not as tied to wheat farming as you thought," Anna smiled into the telephone.

"No, that eases my mind more than you can

know. Frank will be glad to be off the hook." Off the hook, Anna was thinking, wishing there was such a simple solution to the problems mounting in her own life. "Perhaps I didn't marry the wrong brother after all," Cassie said, suddenly getting serious.

"The grass is always greener...." Anna tried to inject a lighter touch.

"Yeah, but it still has to be mowed! I'll send you that recipe for molasses pie. Kevin will love it."

Anna nearly choked on her next words. "I'm sure he will." There was a commotion at Cassie's end and then she was gone in a rush of goodbyes.

SATURDAY DAWNED with one of those sunny clear days that Washington often boasts about. Forgotten was the freakish cold snap with sleet and scattered snow, and the natives joined the hordes of tourists under the bright blue sky to shop and see their city. Anna pulled the draperies back to let the sunshine into her room. She felt reluctant to leave it. If only she could stay forever in its cocoon of enveloping warmth.

Caburn would be back today with Kevin. The knowledge kept her breathless with worry. She had imagined a thousand times over the past hours the look on his face when Caburn had approached him; she imagined his look of shock, the dismay, and wondered what his reaction had been. She wondered, too, if Kevin had asked about her, asked if she knew, asked if his mother knew. In her heart she knew the futility of that. His concern would be all for Janie and their son.

Oh, but she wanted this day to be over, to be erased; she wanted it to be Sunday; she wanted the anxious feeling of approaching doom that was sweeping over her to dissolve. Her mouth kept going dry and she was jumping at every sound.

The telephone rang and she refused to go near it.

Clara Alice answered it in the middle of a ring, but didn't come to give Anna any message, so that she was finally driven from her room to ask. It had only been Lila Hammond on her way to market, wanting to know if they needed anything from the grocer's.

Late in the afternoon Anna dressed in slacks and a warm wool pullover and went for a long walk, to think, she told herself. On her future. But her thoughts were fragmented, full of the past and much on the present, so that none of the anguish she was suffering was eased. She was only peripherally aware of a gentle breeze tousling her hair, of the lowering sun warm on her face, of her feet crushing brown autumn leaves. She walked with her eyes cast down. She came upon a sock. Surely Kevin's. One she had tossed out. She didn't bend to retrieve it, but stepped around it carefully. It was of no use. There was no mate for it. Like there was no mate for her. It was like saying goodbye. There was this stark aching in her heart and she didn't think it would ever go away. Tears were sliding down her cheeks when she turned onto the sidewalk in front of her house.

"Anna...."

She lifted her face. Caburn and another man, a stranger, were standing at her door. Her breath caught in her throat as Caburn came down the steps and took her arm. His face was lined with lack of sleep, his gray eyes filled with kindness and concern as they swept over her. She wanted to fall into his arms, accept his friendship, feel his strength, but the other man was watching her with a quizzical expression on his face. He had a huge powerful head upon a scrawny neck and he limped as he came down the steps toward her.

"This is my boss, Albert Phipps," Caburn said.

Anna thrust out her hand, leaving Phipps to find it and grasp it in his huge one as she used her other to wipe away the dampness on her face. Clara Alice opened the door and, seeing the grim unyielding expressions on the men, took an involuntary step back, for once silent.

"We'd better go in," Phipps said, and Anna felt herself being ushered into her own home between the two men. Phipps was wishing desperately that he had let Caburn handle this himself, but he had wanted to have a look at Anna Nesmith. All of Caburn's conversation, not to mention his reports, were filled with mention of her. Now he could see why. She appeared to have an incredible dignity drawn, he suspected, from an inner resource she didn't even know she had. So this was the woman who had asked good old Francis if he had ever killed anybody. But she looked so tiny and fragile next to Caburn's great hulk....

Anna was acutely aware of sound. It was the fear in her. The soft rustlings as coats were removed and thrown over the back of the sofa, the shuffling of Clara Alice's slippers as she moved nervously from the vestibule, the murmuring of voices as Caburn introduced her to Albert Phipps, the polite refusal of coffee. And all around her, Anna sensed the reticence of officialdom. She curled up in her favorite chair, becalmed in the eye of the storm, waiting it out as though she was in a disembodied dream. Phipps indicated that Clara Alice, too, should sit, and Anna knew this was *the end*. Why else had Caburn brought along his boss? Albert Phipps cleared his throat.

"There's really no easy way to do this," he said. Anna's eyes flew to Caburn. He gave nothing away by his expression. His broad shoulders were hunched, as though ready to spring. The fear in her grew. Phipps had held his pause dramatically until Anna was forced to look at him once again. "I'm sorry to have to tell you that Kevin Nesmith is dead."

Caburn twitched, but no one else moved for several long heartbeats, then Anna got up, meaning to go to Clara Alice, who had turned very white, her old eyes squeezed shut in her round fleshy face. Anna couldn't understand why she felt so leaden, so rubbery. Her gaze burned into Caburn, searching, asking if this was true, asking, "Did you kill him?"

Albert Phipps was shocked. "Nesmith died of natural causes. A heart attack according to our autopsy, at Orly airport in France." He turned to Clara Alice, who was sitting stiffly, her hands clasped to her face, her eyes open now and wild with disbelief. "Are you all right, ma'am?"

"My son is dead?" The words seemed to heave from Clara Alice of their own volition, then she fell back against the sofa, grief stricken, but not crying or making any sound. Caburn moved from the side of Anna's chair swiftly to the front door. An instant later a nurse in starched white bustled in, took Clara Alice's pulse and blood pressure.

"Okay, so far," she said after a moment. Phipps nodded and the nurse moved into the background, taking a seat on the narrow bench in the vestibule, but Phipps signed her into the kitchen, out of earshot.

Anna felt possessed, as if another person was taking over her flesh and nerves. That had to be because her real self was numbed, unable to function. She heard herself asking, "When?"

"Just after he stepped off the airplane from the U.S., Wednesday before last." Phipps was drumming his bony fingers on the sofa arm. "I'm sorry we couldn't tell you earlier. His death stirred up a hornet's nest at State." He looked from Caburn to Anna. "I believe you now know the reason for that."

Anna wasn't listening. She was trying to come to

grips with the timetable. Wednesday. *Wednesday.* That meant...that meant...that she had gone to bed with Caburn while Kevin was lying cold and dead somewhere in France. And Caburn had known it! She could never forgive herself. Or him. Caburn could've told her. He should've told her, instead of playing charades, instead of pretending an investigation. What difference did it make what Kevin had done now that he was dead? Nothing else mattered. Yes...yes, there was something else. She just couldn't get it to come to mind. Pictures were skimming along the surface of her brain. She saw one clearly. It had huge violet eyes. Wife. Kevin's other wife. That was it. Kevin wouldn't have to suffer now for what he had done. Wouldn't have to answer for his actions. The person who possessed her began to scream. "Kevin had no right to die! No right!"

Caburn was at Anna's side at once, sitting on the arm of her chair, feeling like his soul was tearing in two. He stroked her with his good hand, clumsily trying to press her head against his chest with the other, murmuring inconsequential nothings, trying to soothe her. Anna would not be calmed. She was hanging onto a sense of reality by a thread. She pulled away from his solid chest, her eyes wet and filled with an inner horror. "What we did was unconscionable," she moaned.

"What? What did you two do?" Clara Alice's eyes fluttered open and beamed on Anna's face that had gone a flaming red beneath damp lashes. "Oh, I knew it!" Clara Alice gasped. "You never loved Kevin. And now he's dead. You have no respect...." She began to cry then, hard gurgling sobs that made Phipps uncomfortable.

"You won't let me stay here now," Clara Alice was wailing. "You've never liked me. You knew about this. You took my bed...."

Phipps knew he had to put a stop to the old woman. Caburn's eyes were beginning to glitter with more than weariness. "Mrs. Nesmith," he said, raising his gravelly voice above Clara Alice's sniffling, "when your son died we were notified at once. I want you to know how sorry we are. We understand he was only forty. But these things happen and we have no control. Our officials in Paris went through his personal papers, of course, and to our dismay, we learned there was more to your son, well... we found out that he has... had two wives."

It took an instant for Clara Alice to comprehend. Her mouth dropped open. Her sobbing stopped as she rose automatically to her son's defense. In outrage, Clara Alice was almost magnificent. She got to her feet and planted her hands on her hips. "Not my Kevin! He wouldn't. He was devoted to me. To Anna. He was a good son and a good husband."

"To his other wife, yes," Caburn injected bitterly. "Not to Anna—" Phipps silenced him with a look.

"You're just making all this up to cover up something. I knew it the moment I laid eyes on you."

"Now... now... Mrs. Nesmith. Mr. Caburn is only doing his job. We *are* going to have to keep this quiet, though." Phipps's Adam's apple was working furiously.

Anna shook her head. "They're not making it up, Clara. I met her. I met Kevin's other wife." She knew she couldn't keep up this pretense of strength much longer. The other self, the one possessing her, was taking over, driving her into a duskiness, a tunnel where sounds reverberated against the lining of her brain, where there was so little light. "There's a child, too. A little boy. He... he looks just like Kevin." Her voice was almost inaudible now, yet it gained strength for a heartbeat. "Oh, why did he have to die? How can I divorce a dead man?"

Her words electrified Clara Alice, but Anna didn't see. She had come to her feet. She'd had enough of this nightmare. Oddly, her legs wouldn't hold her. She thought she sat down again. It was so dark suddenly that she wondered why no one had turned on the lights. She heard the swishing of a starched skirt, felt hands fumbling with her sweater, her arm, and opened her mouth to protest the needle jabbing into her muscle. And then she felt very warm and free, floating...floating as though she had been released from a prison. Released from the nightmare.

10

DOCTOR MCVEY'S WORDS were still ringing in Caburn's ears. A discreet man favored by State's standards, he had been brought in to examine Anna and briefed as much as Phipps had thought necessary. "You can expect a listless despondency, melancholia and grief; perhaps in her situation, even relief and guilt. I daresay she'll survive. On the other hand, loss of appetite due to trauma and shock...now that's another ball game. If she hasn't eaten in two days' time, bring her in to see me." Caburn fingered the doctor's card. Worry was evident in his face. Blond beard stubble was thick and shadowy on his jaw; his eyes were far back in their sockets, making them look darker and more menacing than they were. He had snatched what sleep he could—when it would come—on Anna's sofa, but he had spent most of the night at her side, watching, praying with his heart in his throat.

Lying in the huge bed beneath the thick mauve coverlet, Anna looked more fragile, more vulnerable than he had ever seen her. She appeared to be wasting away, and on purpose. The enforced inactivity had his muscles bunched up and screaming for relief. He was pacing her bedroom when she woke up.

Anna lay abed, unmoving, tracking him with her eyes. "You always do that when something's on your mind." He stopped in midstride and looked at her. She sounded so weak it scared him. "What's bothering you now? It's all over, isn't it?"

"How do you feel?"

She lifted her hand and let it fall in a helpless gesture back to the bed. "Drugged. I was drugged, wasn't I? I didn't imagine that?"

"You didn't imagine it."

"The way you're looking at me...there *is* something else, isn't there? Something unpleasant."

"I don't want to upset you."

A thin line of sunshine found its way into the room through a crack in the draperies and rippled across Anna's face. She moved up against the headboard to shift the glare from her eyes. Her hair was disheveled but it still had luster, framing her face so that to Caburn she appeared to be all eyes and mouth. Her color was high and he feared she had a fever. He tore his eyes away from her and began to pace the room again.

The ribbon of light now gleamed on her wedding band. It caught Anna's attention. She stared at it for a long futile moment, then twisted it from her finger. "There isn't anything you can say or do that would upset me anymore than I have been. The worst has...." She discovered she was in her pajamas and shoved the ring into her pocket. She had the same feeling as when she had come across Kevin's sock on the sidewalk. Another goodbye, only this one was more final. The fact of his death was sinking in. It left her with a dragging sadness. "If you have any more questions, ask them. Get it over with."

He sat on the edge of her bed and shoved his injured hand through his blond curls, leaving them in disarray. "Are you sure?"

"I'm sure." But she wasn't. She wasn't sure of anything anymore.

"We're still working on Nesmith's calendars. Those curious little marks began in August. Can you think of anything unusual that happened in August?" He took a scrap of paper from his pocket, glancing at it. "On the eleventh, to be exact."

Anna smiled, a slight curving of her lips that did not reach her eyes. "Now I know how a witness feels on the stand. That was so long ago." A lump was forming in her throat. "That was in my other life." She closed her eyes and for a long while didn't speak. "August was hot...and dry. We had no rain...my petunias died...." She was fading off into some world that he didn't know. He wanted to imbue her with his own strength, his own powerful emotions, yank her back to reality.

"Anna...please...think!"

She was thinking. She had stopped taking birth-control pills in August, but what good would it do to dredge that up now? There was no doubt about Kevin's sexual preference anymore. It was called Janie.

Caburn had seen a memory taking shape as her lids flickered. "Well?"

"There's nothing. Are you still looking for black-mailers?"

"We'd like to be able to rule them out. As far as we can tell, he didn't sell the information he was carrying. You were right about that. He was true to his country."

"But not to me."

Pushing her like this was tearing him apart. He watched her lids fall, the lashes lying dark and feathery along her cheek, and could see tears beginning to trickle out beneath them. He wanted to take her into his arms, hold her, feel her soft flesh against his own and knew now was not the time. Not yet. "No, not to you. What were you thinking just a moment ago?"

"It's too personal. It had nothing to do with you or the State Department. It was just an old memory, or wishful thinking."

"I wish you'd let me be the judge of that."

"How's Clara Alice holding up?"

Caburn sighed and looked away. "She's not here."

Anna felt a chill thread its way up her spine. "Where is she?"

She's in Ellicott City. She insisted on meeting Janie and seeing the baby. She's willing—eager—to continue the myth that you're Nesmith's sister, if it means a continuing link with her grandson."

Her eyes went very wide. "That's not fair!"

"I know. There just can't be any publicity on this, Anna. Not only for State's sake, but for your own as well. Janie's dad is a very outspoken retired judge, often in the news. He's thinking about running for political office in Maryland. Things could get messy for all of us if this got out. There'd be a big flap about security measures.... Would this be so hard for you to live with?"

"You mean just keep my marriage to Kevin a secret forever? As if I...as if our marriage never existed?"

"No, not forever. For a little while. Janie will have to be told eventually."

"How long is a little while? What will I tell my colleagues at work? My friends? My dad? You're asking too much of me. Am I supposed to do this for my country?" Anger and sarcasm were giving her a false energy. She swung her legs over the side of the bed, felt her head begin to swim and lay back, an arm thrown over her eyes.

"Tell your dad whatever or as much as you like. Don't say anything at all to your co-workers—"

"Clara Alice could never keep a secret."

"She's a tough old bird in her own way, Anna. She'll keep this one. She wants that grandson."

"And me? What about what I want?" Caburn was not prepared for the sudden venom in her voice and kept silent. Anna turned over and buried her face in her pillow. "What about what I'm suffering? I hurt so badly." Her voice was little more than a husky muffled whisper. She began to cry.

Caburn couldn't help himself. He lay down beside her and pulled her into his arms, holding her, knowing words were useless. The warmth of her, the smell of her filled him with a hunger, a protectiveness; he wanted to possess her, possess everything she was, take away her pain, make her one with him. It was all he could do to keep from telling her that he loved her.

After a long while she stopped sobbing and blew her nose on a tissue. Her throat hurt and she didn't want to talk. She was filled with a myriad of confusing sensations. The pain and self-pity that was all mixed up and belonging to Kevin; the comfort and the aura of strength that came to her from Caburn. He was real, here when she needed him, his arms a haven, and the love she felt echoed in an empty place.

The telephone shrilled and she lifted her head from his chest. "Is it ringing in here? You fixed this extension?"

"Last night," he answered, withdrawing his arm reluctantly so that she could sit up.

It was Clara Alice. "Anna...how're you feeling now?" There was a softness in the voice that had never been evident; gone was the strident, aggressive Clara Alice that Anna knew so well.

'I'm...I'm better." She hardly knew what to say to her mother-in-law now. The circumstances were so utterly off the wall, they added to her confusion.

"Did they tell you? I'm...at Janie's."

Anna felt hot tears swelling beneath her lids once again. She nodded, then realized Clara Alice couldn't see her. "Yes."

"I'm going to stay here. Janie asked me." There

was something proud in Clara Alice's tone. Anna was bereft of words while something seemed to break inside her. "Will you keep on letting Janie think you're...that you're Kevin's sister...? My daughter? For the baby's sake?" Clara Alice paused, her voice almost inaudible. "Anna...*for my sake?*" And in case the answer wasn't one she wanted to hear, she rushed on, giving Anna no opportunity to interrupt. "I know we never got along too well. It...it was my fault. I just wanted to be wanted. I'm only thinking of my grandson, Anna. The stigma. Kevin was wrong to do what he did, but Janie needs me now...." The rush of words trailed off, haltingly, her next comment almost pitiful. "It's been so long since anyone needed me...."

"I—I have to think about it," Anna said, but she knew she had little choice, no choice in the face of Clara Alice's confession.

"I'll call you after Kevin's funeral, then."

Kevin's funeral. She still had that to get through. "Yes," she whispered. "Do that." The receiver slipped from Anna's fingers into her lap. When she made no move to cradle it, Caburn reached over and put it in its place. "There were so many times when I could have used some kindness from Clara Alice," she said sadly. In its way it was another loss. She glanced at Caburn, who was now leaning against the headboard. "I get the feeling I'm not supposed to attend Kevin's funeral."

"Can we talk about this later? After breakfast?" He desperately wanted to get some nourishment into her. He had not fully realized how thin she was getting until he had taken her into his arms. Her eyes were red rimmed, her face ravaged with tears, yet he thought she looked beautiful.

Anna moved unsteadily toward the bathroom and when she reached its threshold she turned back to

glare at Caburn, and some of the spark, the flame
that was intrinsically ingrained in all that she was,
surfaced. "What's left for me? What do I have left to
cling to? Kevin did love me once, and I loved him. . . .
None of you can take that away from me. I won't let
you."

"You can cling to me," he said softly.

"Until you're certain that I won't rock the boat?
Until you're assigned to another case?" The bitterness in her voice was profound, and Caburn knew
that teaching her to trust him, or anyone again, was
going to be the toughest battle he had ever fought.
His weapons would have to be sympathy, con-
straint, humility—none of which he was any too familiar with. It was a battle he meant to win.

"I don't want to take anything away from you . . .
only add. Our destinies are entwined. . . ."

She gave a small sound that passed for laughter.
"Entwined? That's poetic coming from you, Caburn.
You mean all knotted up, don't you? With red tape
from the State Department."

"You've lost a great deal, Anna, but you'll survive."

"It's not the same as living." She closed the bathroom door.

Caburn lifted an arm to cover his powerful profile,
sighing inwardly. *Take it just one step at a time*, he
told himself, already chafing at the tools he had
chosen for this battle.

11

"If I'm supposed to continue this farce that I'm Kevin's sister, they'll expect me at the funeral," Anna insisted from her perch on the arm of her favorite chair.

Phipps was leaning on the back of the sofa; his thigh ached, but he was too troubled to sit. For a brief moment his eyes left Anna and tracked Caburn as he stalked and prowled the room. "That's why I'm here, Mrs. Ne...may I call you Anna?"

"Would you prefer to use my maiden name?" Her voice was soft, filled with a sarcasm that was not lost on Phipps. He had the grace to blush and that made him stammer. His world and work were filled with men. Women were an infernal mystery to him, except for Louise, and she was a mystery to herself.

"I—it's not what you're thinking. It's just that Caburn—" He snapped his mouth shut when Caburn stopped pacing and glared at him. "What I meant...oh, hell. Mrs. Nesmith, we'd prefer it if you didn't go. Funerals have a way of setting off uncontrollable emotions. We're trying to keep a tight lid on this thing."

Anna was becoming angry. "He was *my* husband—unless you can prove otherwise—and I'm going." She was holding her hands clasped tightly in her lap to hide their trembling.

He tried another tack. "If you could just understand our position."

"Mr. Phipps, if you could just understand mine."

He massaged the bridge of his bony nose and sighed. "You win. You will keep a low profile?"

Anna flushed with this small victory. "I'll be with the family."

Phipps winced as he straightened, signaling to Caburn. In the vestibule he whispered in his gravelly voice, lowering it to the decibel of a freight train backing up. "Can't you get Dr. McVey to tell her she's not strong enough to go?"

"I tried that already. She really isn't, you know."

"Damn all determined women," Phipps echoed soulfully. "Well, you've tied into one adamant lady. Keep a handle on her."

"It's my one aim in life," Caburn answered with feeling.

AT THE CEMETERY Anna sat next to Caburn in the back of the limousine provided by the State Department. Kevin was being buried next to Janie's mother. It was very cold and overcast and Caburn was insisting that she wait until the last minute to leave the warmth of the car. She watched through the darkened windows as people emerged from the limousine parked in front of them and gasped involuntarily as Janie Nesmith, clad all in black, was helped to her feet by a stately-looking older man.

"Judge Dickerson," Caburn said. "Janie's dad."

Then Clara Alice emerged, clasping her grandson to her bosom.

Anna leaned her head against the window. She couldn't go through with the charade. "I can't. I can't do it after all. I can't stand up there with them and pretend...." Her thoughts were broken and jagged and she fought the pain of loss. So much had been taken from her. So much. She didn't know how she could bear it. She watched the rites until the flag draping Kevin's coffin was folded and handed to Janie. "Please," she choked. "Take me home."

She was at her worst the remainder of the day. Guilt, sadness and hate merged as a single emotion within her, all of it cloaked by an anger stemming from the fact that she had so little control over the events happening in her life. Caburn refused to leave her. Nothing she could say or do would budge him. In the end she left him to his own devices and holed up in her bedroom with the door locked until dusk, when she burst into the kitchen where Caburn was making hot chocolate.

"I want you to take me to church," she demanded. "Any church, where I can kneel down and pray." Would that God could hear.

There were Wednesday-night services everywhere and Caburn stopped at the first church he came upon that had people milling around. They slipped into a back pew. Anna stayed on her knees during the entire service, oblivious to those around her. In her mind she held her own private burial ceremony, where she surrendered Kevin to whatever spirits, whatever heaven—or hell—there was.

"Feel better?" Caburn shook out her coat and wrapped it around her shoulders as they emerged from the elegant old church, bracing against the wind.

"A little. Could we walk for a while? I'm so wound up."

Caburn tried to offer some consolation, but his own insides, his own thoughts were in turmoil. Phipps was pushing him to close the case. They were beating a dead horse. Nothing was coming of Nesmith's calendars, but Caburn was hanging on. Too, he wanted an official excuse to be with Anna. He had no right, except he felt in his heart he must pursue her. He wasn't sure she would stand for that. It was confusing to him and curious that she seemed to have blocked from her mind the hours they had spent in one another's arms. He wanted her to mention it, make some reference to it, but then, he thought, it was probably only his vanity crying out for recognition. Anna touched him on his arm and he realized she was still waiting for his answer. "Around the block once, maybe you'll work up an appetite."

"I'm so tired of you pushing food at me. When I'm hungry I'll eat."

Her expression was so serious, her tone so practical, he had to smile. Yet he couldn't forget what Dr. McVey had told him, how the body and brain reacted to stress. Anna was surviving on instinct and didn't know it. "A hot bowl of soup couldn't go amiss, and maybe you can keep it down." Twice today he had heard her retching in the bathroom, and only the fact that she was making a superhuman effort to contain her dignity kept him from rushing to her aid.

"Don't you ever give up?" She stopped walking suddenly and grabbed at his arm. "Wait...I know it sounds weird, especially in this cold, but I have a taste for ice cream...."

Caburn's appetite was only for Anna, and the ache he felt could have been declared a famine. He humored her. "Ice cream it is. We'll stop at the grocer's...." He tucked her arm into his, savoring the feel of her against his side.

"Actually, I want one of those big homemade cones stuffed with chocolate chip, the kind they sell at the Old Post Office Pavilion...."

He was taken aback. "But...that's way down on Pennsylvania Avenue."

"I know. But I just have this urgent craving, I can

almost taste it uneaten. I've thrown up so much lately. Maybe my body's crying for some vitamin or chemical."

He hurried her along and ushered her into his car. "Well, if you're going to eat, ice cream isn't all that nourishing. You need red meat, eggs...."

"I want chocolate chip ice cream."

He moaned a little in exasperation. "I'm beginning to think I'm pampering you too much. You're getting stubborn."

"You're not pampering me, you're just doing your job. I overheard Phipps tell you to keep a handle on me."

But Anna had to admit, even if only to herself, and then bury the thought deep within her subconscious, that Caburn's attentions were more than just his work. Love didn't last, no matter what he had said about destinies being entwined. Janie and her son were walking proof of that. Had Kevin lived, they would've been divorced. Being widowed was no different. There was still this awful grief, this awful pain, and Caburn was being kind to her. More than kind. It was all the more reason to keep her guard up. These feelings she had for him that kept gnawing at her and bursting through at all the wrong times would have to be submerged, would have to be bound tightly and never be allowed to surface. She might survive what she was going through once, but never twice. She would accept him as a friend. Nothing more. He had once teased her about being an acquaintance of value. She would hold it to that.

THERE ARE PLACES where death, no matter whose or how quiet, must be recorded, and there are people who demand notification. Insurance companies and mortgage holders are two. To her dismay, Anna learned that Kevin had changed the beneficiary on his insurance policies to Janie. She found that she was left with her home; the credit-life policy that Kevin had bought on the house paid off the remainder of the mortgage. The home in Mission, Kansas, still being rented, had been left to Clara Alice. There was a bare thousand dollars left in their joint checking account and Anna had access to that or she would have been virtually penniless. She had no choice except to return to work.

The Monday following Kevin's funeral she was on the job, filled with a dread born of the future's uncertainty. One of her favorite colleagues, Joyce Ford, looked her up and down. "We heard you'd had a relapse, but you look like death knocked on your door, then backed up."

Anna wanted to say that it had and swallowed her up. Instead she smiled weakly, trying to maintain a facade. "I feel like it, too."

No one mentioned or asked after Kevin, but they never had in the past and Anna didn't bring his name into conversation. Her co-workers were used to her rushing home to Clara Alice each day, so she didn't enlighten them that this, too, had changed. She had always been a very private person, not one to air her problems, so there was no difficulty in maintaining the silence required by State.

Several weeks after Kevin's funeral she received a letter coauthored by Janie and Clara Alice, asking her to come to dinner. Janie thanked her for coming to the funeral. "I think Kevin knows and understands that you would've become friends again," she wrote. Anna declined the invitation, but the letter sent her into such a fit of depression that she lost what little appetite she had regained.

Yet she craved chocolate chip ice cream, and each day after work she went down to the pavilion and bought herself a three-scoop cone before driving home.

At first it was a novelty to go home to the quiet peace and tranquil existence in which Anna found herself. She did the things she wanted to do, when she wanted to do them. She went to movies, read books far into the night and once she had put her house in the order in which she liked it, delighted that it remained that way. Gone was the tension she used to suffer upon arriving home to discover Clara Alice's heavy-handed rearrangement.

Because she was a close neighbor, Anna felt obliged to explain Clara Alice's absence to Lila Hammond. She told her only as much as she dared, swearing the older woman to secrecy. They were sharing a cup of tea in Anna's tiny kitchen, and Lila's old face filled with compassion.

"What you have to do now is look to the future. Forget the past. Forget the parts of the past that have hurt you. Just remember the good things. I'll tell you something. Ace spent a lot of time in the Arctic before I could join him, and those Eskimos have a custom of sharing their women. Ace wasn't one to do without. A thousand times I wanted to ask...but I didn't. I'm glad now that I never raised that question between us. I doubted him often, but I never doubted myself. Believe that you'll make it, and you will."

Anna sighed. "Sometimes it's so hard for me to just hold my head up."

Lila laughed. "Your neck will do that for you. Just keep your eyes open."

It felt good to have another woman to talk to, especially one as sympathetic as Lila, and just when Anna was feeling courageous enough to really open up and bare her soul, Lila's older sister fell and broke her hip. Lila closed up her house and went to Florida. It was another goodbye.

But Caburn never let her feel alone, though he protested vehemently about her breach of security. "If you want to talk to someone, talk to me," he told her one night when he'd dropped in, as he frequently did, to see her.

Anna squared her shoulders and sat motionless, her posturing enhancing the delicate balance of her head upon her slender neck. "What's done is done. Besides, Lila's gone now."

"Don't look so forlorn, I'm here, and I have a good listening ear."

"It's not the same," she reasoned. "You're not a woman."

"Thank God for that," he laughed.

"It's not funny."

He wanted to be all things to her, her friend, her protector, her lover. "Are you trying to pick a fight with me?"

"Would it do any good?"

"Only if you promise to make up...."

His voice caressed her, making her tremble. He had not made any move to touch her sexually, but the desire was there, in his voice, in his eyes. She had tried to ignore it, but as she recovered from her grief, the passion they had once shared loomed between them, pulsating in the very air they breathed, a living thing, impossible not to acknowledge.

"It's getting late," she said shakily, her lips parting in a breathless little moue. She couldn't take her eyes from him.

The need to be wanted, to be loved, to give of herself was strong in Anna. The foundations in her life had quivered and fallen; she needed to build them up again, mend the wreckage of her life. She just couldn't sit around in dust and ashes and let her life get away from her. Sometimes she felt so small and insignificant, but when she was with Caburn, her heart soared; she felt alive and the humiliation she felt in the face of Kevin's betrayal melted away. She wanted Caburn in every way a woman wants a man.

Their conversation was inane on the surface, though the language their bodies communicated was that of virtuosos, knowledgeable in the art of love. Vertigo was upon Anna again, but of a different kind than that which often sent her running to the bathroom for relief. She was sinking deeper and deeper into a quicksand that throbbed and pulsed with erotic energy. She was unable to take a breath, listening with her eyes as well as her ears... waiting....

She told herself that if he asked, if he voiced the question, she would say no, though the sensual raptness she was feeling was utterly beyond her control.

Caburn sensed in her these dueling forces. He was a virile man, too long without a woman. Blood was pounding in his ears. "I'm staying the night," he said with quiet force, and waited for her to dispute him... hoping....

Her hand made that delicate gesture of resignation that he was coming to know so well. "It's wrong," she said, her eyes huge and glistening and filled with a wistfulness. And then her voice dropped to a whisper. "But I want you to stay."

He locked up the house, turned out the lights, and in the bedroom their hands moved with such urgency on each other that she could not recall coming out of her clothes. "It's just lust," she whispered, those words the closest she could come to voicing denial.

He stroked the small of her back. "Don't put a name to it, Anna. Don't worry about anything. Let's just enjoy each other."

At first her kisses were reticent until his darting

tongue thrust past her lips and her heart raced with excitement. She became a captive for his pleasure. Their hands and mouths were everywhere on each other, exploring in ardent, undulating, seemingly insatiable passion. They wanted each other equally, their tongues playing together while husky moans and throaty utterances drowned in sensual glee, and everything flew out of Anna's mind like leaves swirling and scattering before a high wind.

As their passion accelerated, driving toward ecstasy, Caburn's hands and fingers prepared her, intent on bringing Anna with him, intent on making her soar. Anna wanted the mounting pleasure to go on and on. It was like a reprieve, an end to a fast, a banquet, a carnal provocative feast and she was the only partaker.

This was not a separate being who was tasting him in her mouth. This was Anna. Herself. The heat radiating from her was not that which had been sparked for another. Caburn knew it and the knowledge was more inflammatory than her undulating hips. He kissed the valley between her breasts, her nipples, his hands caressing her torso, exploring her silken thighs until she was moving with the involuntary pounding rhythm of her heart. The blood in her veins ran hot, pooling between her thighs like the surging tide of a thunderous sea.

Then his hands held her hips and lifted them and hard flesh entered her. Anna thrust her hips forward, participating. She was giving and taking. Her delicate fingers moved slowly up over his back, caressing the muscles, toying with the hair on the nape of his neck. She felt his flesh within her grow harder and slip deeper into her. She locked her fingers around Caburn's neck and pulled his head down and opened her mouth to his. All her desire was aroused. She was woman. And she was being loved for being that woman. She allowed herself a second to think of the past, finding nothing there that had matched this, that could match the astonishing sensations that were burning within her now.

Caburn spoke with his mouth just touching hers. "I've wanted you like this since the moment I saw you...wanted all of you, with no one between us...." And then his possession was complete, their union explosive, the surging tide rose higher, insatiable, her thighs climbing with it, seeking an outlet behind the dam. Anna cried out, the soft sound like an erotic lure, and he surrendered, sinking into the whorling tempest that was the woman beneath him....

And even as they untangled arms and legs, Anna could still feel his hands on her everywhere, wanting all of her, and it was long minutes before she became aware of cooling air on her sweat-drenched body.

In the languid aftermath of lovemaking her mind raced forward with a timorous spark of determination. If a man like Caburn could love her, make love to her as he had and accept what she had offered, there was hope. She determined that she would learn to handle her money, learn to handle her fear of being alone, and she would go to the doctor to learn why she hadn't conceived. Knowing the reason would help her accept and face the fact. She had one attribute, Anna knew, that had never failed her...perseverance.

She meant to talk, to tell Caburn all that she was feeling, but her knotted nerves were soothed, and when he pulled her into his arms, resting her head on his shoulder, she closed her eyes and plunged into a deep dreamless sleep.

In the morning she woke lying snuggled against his back, smiling, thinking that a measure of equilibrium had been restored to her life, but Nature would have her revenge. As Anna threw the covers back and lowered her legs over the bed, her vision blurred; blood rose to heat her face, causing a thin bead of perspiration on her forehead, and a stabbing threat of nausea became a reality. She raced to the bathroom trailing shredded dignity, tattered perseverance and a touch of ignominy.

It was a few minutes later that she became aware of Caburn bending over her. "Oh, get out of here, please."

"You're sick. Did I hurt you last night?" He grabbed a cloth, wrung it with cool water and put it on her neck.

"No, just too much rich food, that's all, too much excitement. It's over for this morning, anyway," she said, straightening.

Caburn helped her back to bed with a worried shake of his head.

"This has been going on far too long." Over Anna's protests, and making bald use of his credentials, he located Dr. McVey.

"Is this the same woman I saw four or five weeks ago?" Dr. McVey asked after hearing Caburn out.

"Yes, but she's still throwing up. She's getting so thin...."

Dr. McVey sighed, wanting to get back to his breakfast. "Anxiety is a real illness, Mr. Caburn, having symptoms that range from increased heartbeat, perspiration, stomach cramps and blurred vision...physiological, but very real. Your girl has it.... You're not giving her time to cope with the trauma she's been facing. She's eating?"

"Now and again. Listen, damn it! I want to know what can be done now! She's sick."

"There are some deep breathing exercises...."

Caburn listened, practiced a moment, hung up and turned to Anna.

"Truly, I feel fine now," she told him, but humored him and followed his instructions. "You know, you look funny, standing there naked, showing me how to breathe in and out."

He smiled and sat on the bed next to her. "If you're feeling all that better, I can get unfunny in a hurry."

"Are you bragging? Or promising?" she asked softly, letting her eyes trail over his magnificent body, noting that he was on the verge of arousal. She could feel the beating of her heart, oddly magnified in the quiet. Small early-dawn sounds drifted in to them from the street outside; wind rustling bare twigs against a near window, a dog barking, a car door slamming.

He pulled the covers back and slid in beside her. "I don't usually get up this early," he said.

"Me neither," she answered, welcoming him in.

Later as light filtered into the room in thin cool bars across the bed, Anna lay stretched back with her hands behind her head and knees bent. She glanced over at Caburn and found his gray eyes blazing at her. "What are you thinking?"

"You first," he said.

"You really want to know?"

He leaned over, kissing her gently on her lips. "I really want to know."

She expelled a soft breath. "For the first time in my life I feel complete. It's not just the sex, though I can't discount it. Maybe it's the catalyst. I just don't feel so much like a lump of dead clay anymore. I always thought Kevin was perfect. That's what caught me so off guard. He was human and weak. That's what I was thinking...." Her voice trailed off. "And you?"

"That we're going to be late for work if we don't get out of this bed. That I'm greedy for you...." He had a prescience of boundaries; hers of pride, bruised, but healing; his, a kind of cynicism that had never let a woman wholly penetrate the man he was...until Anna. It would take some getting used to.

She pressed his hand, now almost healed, to her lips. "I'll make coffee while you shower. It's kind of nice to lie in bed and do things, but I'm a single working woman again, and my sole support." She moved from the warmth of the bed and pulled on a robe. And as she went to make breakfast, she was thinking that she hadn't gotten up yet, that she was having a happy dream.

PHIPPS DRUMMED HIS FINGERS on the Formica table top in the small Pilots' Association cafeteria and peered hard at Caburn, who sat glumly across from him, looking weary and fatigued. "Got the splints off your hand, I see. Healed up okay?"

Caburn flexed his fingers, then dug around in his pockets for his pipe and tobacco. "Yeah, a little stiff in the cold is all." His eyes darkened suddenly. "Could you stop that damned drumming? It's driving me crazy."

He was surprised at the outburst. Phipps's hands went very still. "You're on edge, my friend," he said softly. "Too much so. Perhaps you need a vacation. You're not doing yourself or the department any good like this."

Caburn went slightly pink behind his ears. "Anna Nesmith got a raw deal...."

"We're back to the Nesmith woman again, are we? She complaining?" Phipps's great head wobbled on his neck. "Listen, Francis, there's nothing like dying to put someone at a disadvantage. There's no way we can interfere with the insurance." He gave a short bray that passed for a laugh. "They're bigger than State, maybe even Defense. Why don't you just marry the girl? That'd take care of it. Then, just maybe...you'd get back to work. Real work. Take it from me, you're falling in love, and once past all this shilly-shallying...you know, where your heart acts funny and you can't control your, er, well, you know, things will be all right."

"Did I ask you for advice? Are you running a lovelorn column or something?" Caburn snapped, the tension around his lips growing more taut. "Anna's not complaining. I don't think she knows how to."

"You're sleeping with her, aren't you?"

Caburn looked away, then back at his boss. "I'm rebound material, that's all. She's had a low blow."

"My, my...we are sensitive, aren't we?" Phipps leaned forward suddenly, his shoulders jerking inelegantly. "Listen, Francis, we're going to have to close this case soon—officially. Just thought you'd like to know."

"What about cryptanalysis? They ever get anything on those calendars and date books?"

"Nope, and they have bigger fish to fry right now. A lot is going down in the Middle East.... I can't hold them on a case that's virtually dead. Nesmith was a bigamist. That's the long and short of it."

His expression grim, Caburn leaned toward his boss. "It means something, damn it! Nesmith was a precise organized man. Every little thing in his life kept in its place, including his wives. I don't like leaving loose ends around. Ask them to work on it...spare time." He almost said please.

"I'll ask, that's the most I can do. Now we'd better get back to Foggy Bottom. State Department security having coffee breaks so near embassy row makes people nervous."

12

THERE WERE PERIODS of time in her life when Anna grieved for Kevin, for the man that had once, early in their marriage, belonged exclusively to her. And there were times when she hated him, when she was filled with a sense of unfairness... usually when she was attempting to balance her budget or stretch her salary to include some inexpensive item she dearly wanted. But these miserable moments came less and less as the days and weeks passed.

She was thrilled with the attention she received from Caburn. She loved him. When she was with him she had a sense of self-worth far beyond any she had ever experienced. He needed her, wanted her in a way Kevin never had. Sometimes when she caught him looking at her, the intense expression on his face literally took her breath away. When he was near, in the same room, the temptation to touch him was so great, the sensations so troublesome all she could think of was how much she wanted to make love to him.

Christmas was hard upon them and Anna felt as though she had to make up for lost time. She had been in such an emotional fugue that Thanksgiving had come and gone without her knowing. Christmas was going to be different. She planned it to be the season that separated her old life from her new.

She left the artificial tree that Kevin had always insisted upon in the attic and bought a tiny, inexpensive but real tree, which filled the house with evergreen fragrance. She hung ribbon-tied bunches of mistletoe atop every door and signed all of her Christmas cards "Love, Anna," with no mention of Kevin. Let them think what they will, she thought, and to heck with the State Department.

She had one bad moment. She called her dad, inviting him to Washington, feeling that now more than ever she could understand his loneliness. He declined. "I've been invited over to a widow friend's I've been seeing," he said.

A widow friend. It sounded like a curse. Anna had almost screamed that she was a widow, too. It made her think... all the wrong thoughts probably, but she wasn't certain of Caburn for the holidays. He had family to go home to. It took her days to build up the courage to ask him his plans.

He gave her one of his warm smiles that took the harsh edge from his features. "You're my Christmas."

"But you have family. Won't your mother be expecting you?" She was thinking of Cassie.

He sighed unexpectedly, letting her see a little deeper into his past, his heart. "I'm a third wheel. It seems to cause tension when I go home on holidays. During harvest and sowing we're busy from sunup to sundown, so I go home then, when I can get away."

The fear of being alone began to recede, but another terror took its place. She was terrified of losing Caburn, to an accident, heart attack, new diseases, and there seemed to be one discovered every day.

They were having dinner at a samurai steak house in a Georgetown mall. "Do you carry a gun?" she asked.

Caburn sputtered into his hot rice wine. "Hell, no! What kind of question is that?"

"How do you keep safe? Sometimes you're gone for days without telling me where you are or where you've been. Is investigative work dangerous?"

"Only when I meet women like you."

Her thick fringe of lashes narrowed to slits. "I suppose you're lumping me with your friend, Rose," she said icily.

"Rose? Who's Rose? You're the only woman in my life," he said in a throaty timbre, tilting her head so that he could plant a warm kiss on the delicate curve of her ear.

Anna felt a monumental force pressing against her breasts. "It can't last, can it? The way we want each other?"

"We might try taking vitamins...."

Her face went pink. "Can't you ever be serious?"

He studied her face for a long enigmatic moment. "I want you more than any woman I've ever known. I think that's serious." He thought she was clinging to him because she had no other, because she was bruised, not yet whole.

Anna waited for him to go on. He didn't and it was the first inkling she had that he might be suffering a torment of his own, though she couldn't imagine what it might be. He had everything.

"I'm having some friends in for Christmas Eve," he announced. "It's sort of a yearly thing. I cook a mean steak, but vegetables, unless out of a can, are beyond my expertise. Care to help me out?"

Her eyes widened in surprise. In many ways they had grown very close, but this was the first time Caburn had invited her into his home, his territory. His wanting her there made her feel gloriously warm all over. "I'd love to." A thought nagged her. "Do...do they know about me? About...?"

"They all work with me, so it's possible, but they'll have the good manners not to embarrass you."

"I wasn't thinking of myself."

Caburn assumed a look of impassivity. "Oh, of me, then?"

"I'm always thinking of you," Anna replied innocently. Caburn's heart soared.

WORK IN THE NATION'S CAPITOL slowed to a standstill the weeks before Christmas. Anna took several extra days off along with her holidays, making an appointment to see her own doctor. State's Dr. McVey might be right about trauma and anxiety, but Anna was more comfortable discussing her problems with her own physician, Dr. Oldham. There was always in the back of her mind the fact that Dr. McVey belonged to State. Whatever he discovered about her would be available to Phipps and Caburn. Infertility was her personal problem, not an item she wanted to share. Besides, seeing Dr. Oldham before the end of the year was like getting a jump on her New Year's resolutions.

Fully dressed after the examination, she busied herself with the clasp on her purse so that she did not have to meet Dr. Oldham's eyes. Her courage hadn't failed her, but it was a bit wobbly.

He was leaning back in his leather chair, his fingers steepled, gazing at her from beneath bushy gray brows. He was a kind man, shrewd in the ways of the human condition. In his thirty years of practice he had seen and heard all manner of suffering, relieving what he could, when he could. "Your problem is in your mind, not in your body, Anna," he said kindly.

She had not expected him to be judgmental on this issue. She felt put upon and not a little defensive. "It's not in my mind. I want to know why my body isn't working right." It didn't seem fair that she was getting a verdict with him sitting there watching her face, watching all her emotions spill out. She glanced up and found to her amazement that there was a trace of a smile on his lips.

"Who said it's not working? You're about as pregnant as any woman I've ever examined."

She was sure she hadn't heard right. "Pardon?"

"You're going to have a baby. Near as I can tell you're six to ten weeks along. I could be more certain if you hadn't lost so much weight since I saw you last. You say you stopped birth control in August?"

"Yes," she choked, "but I didn't have a period afterward...."

"That's nothing unusual, and what with the trouble you've been through...." He cleared his throat.

Anna was thinking, *six to ten weeks*. The timing was critical. Ten weeks pregnant would make Kevin the father of her child. Six weeks—Caburn. The office suddenly became oppressive, the walls closing in on her. She made as if to stand and found her legs wouldn't hold her. The swirl of conflicting emotions she felt turned in on themselves like a tightly coiled rope. She shook her head disbelievingly, her hands falling helplessly into her lap.

"Dr. Oldham...." Her voice lost itself unexpectedly in a whisper. My husband died and I...." She lifted her eyes and they were filled with panic. "Is there anyway you can tell which...I mean who...if there was another man besides my husband...who the father of my baby is?"

He looked surprised, but erased it from his expression at once, shaking his head. "If you can recall the exact day that you went with each man...?"

"I can! The last time with Kevin was two days after my birthday, October 3rd...." She pressed her fingertips to her temples, thinking...trying to remember the day Caburn had walked into her life, trying to remember the Sunday that Janie had.... "The other man, I mean, the other time was the *last* Sunday in October." She looked at Dr. Oldham with hope in her eyes. He was shaking his head.

"You're speaking of a span of only three...four weeks. You can count," he suggested. "The human gestation period is 280 days, the average delivery date from conception about 266. And, right now, I'd say your delivery date is somewhere in June or July. Sooner, perhaps."

Anna's heart sank. "But...but you mean wait until the baby is born and count backward! What about blood tests?"

"Anna...." Dr. Oldham spread his hands enigmatically. "Blood tests only rule out who the father can be—they don't prove conclusively who *is*."

Anna stumbled from Dr. Oldham's office. This couldn't be happening to her. Not like this. It wasn't how she had planned approaching motherhood at all. She had to arrive at decisions, make preparations; the trouble was, she couldn't do anything but wait.

All Christmas week she tried to suspend her worries, her anxiety, so that she could get through the party Caburn had planned. She wished, knowing it was futile, for someone to talk to. If only her mother had not died. If only she and Clara Alice had been close, or Lila was home from Florida. If only Cassie and Caburn had not.... In her mind's eye she could see herself telling Caburn: *Listen, darling, I have exciting news. I'm having a baby. It may or may not be yours....*

Oh, yeah? I've heard that one before. Cassie tried it.

But slowly the unease she felt gave way to exultation. She was having a baby! That she wanted it to be Caburn's baby so bad she could taste it was a thing she would have to learn to live with.

CABURN'S HOUSE WAS OLD, two story, built of wood and very narrow, yet inside it had the ambiance of a sun-drenched Mediterranean island with earthy pastel tones and oversized pottery. Anna had expected it to be far more masculine with the starkness that sometimes seemed to edge itself around his personality.

The walls were painted cream and the man-size lounges covered in teal cotton. Roman shades of the same stone-washed fabric added softness along a wall of big windows that overlooked a garden lush with evergreen trees and shrubs. Peach-and-gray tones highlighted a round marble-top table with a pickled wood pedestal, carved in a pineapple shape. There was recessed lighting and Chippendale-styled side chairs and, beneath it all, a pale dhurrie rug with exotic North African motifs. The very modern kitchen gave her a twinge of envy. The dining area continued the Mediterranean ambiance, with floors done in soft red tiles and graced by huge earthenware pottery. It was all airy and mellow.

He took her on a tour of the upstairs bedrooms and when they came to his, he slipped his arm around her waist. "I have to sleep in that big old bed all by myself every night," he crooned softly in her ear.

She was suddenly very shy in his presence. Being pregnant shouldn't make a difference, but it did somehow. "You should've written Santa a letter," she answered teasingly. "He might have thought to put a warmer in your stocking."

Caburn thought Anna looked radiant. She was wearing a slender, capped-sleeved, soft pink sheath trimmed with tiny seed pearls around the collar. Her dark hair framed her face perfectly and her eyes were glowing with some unidentified euphoria. He was once again struck by her delicate beauty. It made his loins ache. He felt vibrations from her that transmitted a serene invisible power celebrating itself and sensed that he was outside of it, whatever the cause. It brought on a familiar outcast feeling.

"A bed warmer would be nice," he said. "The one I have in mind is exquisitely sensual and runs her fingertips along my back at the most intimate moments...."

Anna gave a soft laugh, looking at him with new eyes, measuring.... Would her child be like him? Blond hair going to curl, moody gray eyes that could blaze with anger or gleam with tenderness? The shape of his mouth would look wonderful on a girl. Without the mustache, of course. Her brown eyes were opaque, her thick dark lashes shielding her thoughts. "I've noticed that when your mind is on sex, you can't seem to think of anything else. If we stay up here, your friends are not going to get any food." She took his hand, pulling him down the narrow stairs, back to the kitchen.

"Switches, that's what ought to be in your stocking," he said with little grace, voicing his disappointment.

Behind the kitchen was a latticed enclosed porch where Caburn announced he would cook the steaks. He put charcoal to burn down in a brazier, then managed to stay underfoot in the kitchen, hovering near her, until his guests began to arrive. He always had some excuse: to retie her apron sash, to show her where to find a knife when she already had her hand in the drawer, or to pull out a pot from beneath the sink just when she had to be there to wash and peel potatoes. She was at all times very aware of him, of his solid length, his after-shave, the sultry gleam in his eyes. Done on purpose, she was certain, and driving her to distraction. She was almost, but not quite, relieved when the doorbell pealed.

The next few minutes were caught up in the flurry of introductions. Jack Evans was a short sturdy man with a receding hairline that gave way incongruously to a mop of brown hair. His wife, Nancy, was a slender brunette with flashing green eyes and a bow mouth given to smiling. Sophia Marshal was as rotund as her husband, James, was thin. Her skin was flawless and she wore a mane of tawny hair tied back with a bright red ribbon. "Well, Caburn's Christmas elf is a real improvement over last year's, especially if she can cook, and the smells coming from the kitchen say she can."

"Oh? Who was the elf last year? Rose?" Anna asked with sly solicitation, ignoring the glare Caburn dispensed her.

"No. Me," said a tall aristocratic woman crowding in behind the other couples. "I'm Louise Phipps, the boss's wife." She smiled ever so slightly at Sophia. Someone had once commented to Louise that she favored Katharine Hepburn, and her style—schoolmarmish, high-necked blouses, loosely knotted chignon, haughty air—all emphasized that compliment. "You're forgiven, Sophia...in the spirit of Christmas," she said with a gallant sweep of long manicured fingers.

Anna's smile was a bit distorted when Albert Phipps joined them, but Caburn sidled up to her, putting his arm around her shoulder protectively, and there was no awkward moment. Phipps wanted to know how she'd been getting along, and she was able to answer him with composure.

Nancy Evans played the accordion. Her husband, Jack's, contribution to the evening was to make eggnog from the ground up. "You have to sip lightly on the stuff," Nancy warned. "Jack thinks adding a quart of rum makes him an expert."

After only a few minutes it was obvious to Anna

that the group were friends of long-standing. They picked and nagged at one another good-naturedly. Caburn had, by some invisible signal, communicated that she was special, and the women took her in—testing her, Anna was sure, to see if she fit into their tight little group.

"You didn't have to come looking so downright elegant," Sophia admonished. "Louise usually decorates the atmosphere for us."

"An accident," Anna laughed. "Should I spill something on myself?"

"Not this time. Eat your heart out, Louise."

The men rallied around the brazier on the back porch with a warming brew to chase away the chill, and the women congregated in the kitchen around Anna. Sophia set the table, Nancy played the accordion, Louise sang in a lovely contralto voice while Anna, feeling wonderful, put the finishing touches to dinner. She had not experienced such a happy magical Chrismas Eve since she was a child.

Jack's eggnog was potent and it loosened tongues, so that during dinner conversation flowed as thick as the rum-filled punch.

"Oh, James suffers from the delusion that all people are created equally interesting."

"It's true, I've never met a boor."

"Only because you don't stay in one place long enough."

"This asparagus is delicious, but I only want the recipe for the sauce. On Jack's salary, I can't afford asparagus."

"You afford everything else. What about that day you spent at Elizabeth Arden's?"

"An emergency. Your mother was coming."

"How's target practice, Louise? Improving any?"

"My aim is as accurate as necessary...isn't it, dear?"

"You can't get Caburn to sit next to a window in an airplane. He goes white."

"I'm a man of earthy pleasures, that means keeping my feet firmly on the ground."

"Play 'O Little Town of Bethlehem' first, Nancy. It's the only one I know all the way through...."

IT WAS CLOSE to midnight before the party broke up with jokes about getting home before Santa's arrival. The sky was clear, filled with stars, the air crisp and cold. Because it seemed so right, Anna leaned with no hesitation into Caburn's circling arms as they watched the last car pull away from the curb.

"It was a wonderful evening," she murmured. "The best Christmas Eve I've ever had. All that singing...I'm hoarse." She was more than hoarse. She was feeling Caburn's body contoured on hers; his chest pressed against her back, his thighs lightly touching her, but pressing nevertheless so that she could sense the beginning of his arousal. She ran her fingertips over the arm that rested just beneath her breasts and felt him shiver, felt his arousal taking more shape. Her breath clotted in her throat while the dilemma of her pregnancy began once again to rise into her conscience.

He touched his face to the side of her head, his lips at her ear, his breath wafting warm. "Your best Christmas Eve ever? Even when you were a little girl?"

Her fingers plucked at a silky blond hair on his forearm. "I was thinking about that earlier. Even then."

His lips moved lightly on the sweet circle of her ear. "It made me feel good to see you so gay tonight." The picture he had of her in his mind all evening—of her radiance, her unique beauty, the graceful way she moved—he doubted would ever fade, no matter how long he lived. He felt her tremble. "You're getting cold."

She wanted to say she never felt the cold when she was in his arms. Instead, when he released her, she followed him into the house and took a seat a small distance away from him on the oversized sofa. She kicked off her shoes, curling her feet beneath her while one arm trailed along the back of the sofa where she picked at an imaginary thread. "It was a fun group of people. I liked them." Her eyes were wide open with the taut clean flesh of her face shadowy in the glow of a flickering candle about to meet its end. "I used to wish for times like these, friends like yours when Kevin and I—I'm sorry. I'm sure you don't want to hear any of that."

In truth, Caburn didn't. He wanted to think of Anna as his, wholly and unconditionally. He didn't want to think of any man touching her, loving her as he had, as he did. "I don't mind," he said. "I'm glad that you feel comfortable enough with me to talk about it."

"I don't like talking about him though; it still hurts. And sometimes I can't keep from wondering what I did wrong, what part of me wasn't woman enough for him...." Her voice trailed off and she dropped her eyes, hiding the pain, feeling all at once a strangeness in her body—her pregnant body.

"Anna...." The way he said her name was a caress that held remembrance of the hours they had spent in love. His thick hand came to her chin, tilting it to face him; her eyes fluttered open only narrowly and she kept them cast down, so that all she could see were the thin white scars on his fingers. She was reminded that they were there because of her. "You're enough woman for me. All that you are, I want. Will you stay the night with me?"

She pulled back, freeing her chin from his fingers.

"No." She couldn't miss the disappointment that sped across his features, and felt obliged to explain. "It's not that I don't want to." *It's because I'm having a baby, you see, and I don't know whose.* "It's just that this is my first Christmas alone...oh, I'm saying this all wrong. What I mean is, I bought a real tree—" she flailed her hand "—and you don't even have one at all...." She lifted her face, her gaze meeting his, bold and shy at the same time. "When you take me home, you...you can stay, if you want."

She held her breath, waiting for his answer. The candle on the table snuffed out, filling the warm air with the smell of hot tallow, leaving only shadows from a recessed light. Her heart and soul clutched at her secret, feeling as dark and shadowy as the room.

"I think not." Caburn knew he could not, would not ever make love to Anna in her home, in her bed again. He had come too far in his relationship with her. Kevin Nesmith's ghost was in that house, and he hadn't the power to exorcise it. He felt again a sense of undoing, thinking that Anna was his on rebound, that her suffering was all that had made her come into his arms.

Yet he could not give up so easily something he wanted so badly. He stood up, turning away from her casually to adjust his trousers lest she see the effect she had on him. "I'll get your coat," he said. He heard Anna's disappointed sigh and smiled inwardly. He planned on getting more than her coat tonight, but the man in him, the persnickety human frailty that made him male and stubborn, wouldn't let him reveal that plan.

Anna rode beside him in the car in a blur of emotions. Every conversation ended awkwardly until she gave up, pulling her coat around her for warmth as they sailed through the silent Washington streets. She was filled with regret. What was a spindly old evergreen compared to Caburn? She couldn't snuggle up to a tree. She put the fact of her pregnancy clear out of her mind.

"I could make us coffee," she told him once they were inside her house, in an attempt to delay his departure.

"I'm full to the brim with coffee. Don't take off your coat."

"I beg your—". She stopped in midsentence. Caburn was striding toward her two-foot tree. He searched beneath the table it sat upon in front of the window, found the plug for the lights, gave it a yank, and wrapped the cord around the stand.

"You don't mind if I borrow your tree, do you?" He moved across the living room, into the foyer and out the door, angel hair from the tiny branches waving, with Anna trailing speechless behind him. He placed it carefully upright on the back seat of his car. "Now—" he said, turning to her "—did you want to pack a bag? A nightgown, which you'll have no use for, toothbrush? Perhaps a change of clothes?"

Her tongue was stuck to the roof of her mouth while her heart thudded unmercifully against the wall of her chest. Caburn held the car door open and indicated the tree. "That was your reason for saying no?"

Somehow her tongue worked loose. "Yes...yes, it was."

"Merry Christmas...?" There was a mere trace of a smile below his mustache.

"Merry Christmas," she returned throatily.

13

THE TINY TREE survived its ride in the back seat. But so much was racing through her mind, Anna almost didn't in the front.

They decided that the marble-topped table was the best place to put the tree. Baubles and trinkets had to be readjusted, the angel hair fluffed, an extension cord found. Anna was trembling with anticipation of the coming hours, yet a kind of unwilling trepidation kept nudging her. Each time Caburn tried to lead her to the bedroom she found some excuse; an ashtray was filled to overflowing and needed emptying; there was candle wax to be removed from a table; a trinket on the tree needed to be moved for better display. Exasperated, finally Caburn grabbed her shoulders, holding her still as he examined her features.

Her eyes were filled with an indefinable luminescence that seduced him as much as her lips and hands had ever done. Yet there was mystery locked in their depths. He shrugged away the wretched thought that she was hiding something from him. "This is silly. You're putting me off. It's not like this is our first time together. Have you tired of me so soon? Have I said or done something wrong?" He pulled her to his taut belly so there was no mistaking the feel of his swelling erection. "I need you, Anna, and I can't wait much longer. Every time I came near you tonight, a certain part of me had a mind of its own and I was afraid I'd embarrass myself."

"I see... feel what you mean," she said with a shaky laugh, very much aware of him.

Emboldened, he began to lead her upstairs to his bedroom, one arm circling her slender waist. She held back at the threshold. "I'm not sure...."

His passion was building at such a fiery rate, it was in him to speak sharply, but he forced a calmness he didn't feel. "Tell me what's bothering you."

"It's... we... it's like going to a motel!"

Appalled, a guttural moan escaped Caburn's lips. "Anna. This is my home...." He was at a loss for more words.

"How many women have you brought here?"

"None. Ever. You're the first... I've always... well, this is my special place—it's where I dream, where I think. I don't like intruders here, leaving their scent, their auras. Hell, I can't explain it."

She averted her face, staring hard at the bed. "Not even Rose?"

"Especially not Rose. I never even had a chance to date her. You saw to that, if you'll put your mind to remembering."

She smiled hesitantly. "Is that true? The call you had me make was to break your first date?"

He didn't dare turn on the overhead light, moving reluctantly away from her to switch on the bedside lamp. Deliberately he began to unbutton his shirt, loosen his belt. He understood. She was struggling for self-confidence, afraid to trust. He chose his words carefully, not looking directly at her, but keeping her stiff posture within his peripheral vision. "I've had other women, Anna. I didn't get to be thirty-eight without enjoying my sexuality. You've had another man, maybe men, for all I know. We're coming into this even stephen...."

"I've only had Kevin."

One too many, he thought, wishing she hadn't

brought Nesmith's name into conversation. "Do you want me to take you home?"

Stricken, she studied him a moment. "No."

Caburn suddenly realized his hands had been tightly balled into fists. He flexed his fingers and held them out to her. "Well then," he said softly, "come over here and let me undress you."

They had a halting beginning, yet it washed over Anna at once—that feeling of being complete the moment Caburn's hot flesh touched hers beneath the coverlet. It made her so giddy she thought she'd cry and was only able to swallow the lump in her throat because his hands and his mouth were creating a longing in her that demanded utter attention.

His lips were feverish, his hands everywhere, his throaty moans filled with sensual pleasure so that, if she didn't stop him, it would all be over soon. Too soon. She ran her fingers through his blond curls, letting her hands fall to each side of his face, and pulled him up. "Please..." she whispered. "Let me make love to you...let me...."

He became instantly still and for a terrible few seconds Anna thought she had repulsed him. "I just want to make you feel the way I do."

He moved off her and lay on his back, but keeping his arm crooked around her and his hand moving in feathery strokes on her hip. "You're going to make me suffer unbearably."

She raised up on an elbow and pressed warm moist lips to his eyelids. "Isn't it a wonderful kind of suffering?"

Caburn knew that he was a man women wanted. They wanted *him* to make love to them, make them feel cherished, as if there were an essence of himself that could be showered on their bodies, yet they gave him nothing beyond physical satisfaction. That Anna wanted to touch him thus, make love to him, was an unexpected gift. When her lips, feeling like dew-moist velvet, touched his eyelids, he shuddered with the exquisiteness of it all.

Her hands crept over him, her lips descending, and when her tongue flicked out to touch his nipple buried in blond hair, the sensation was so intensely unnerving he almost stopped her; then his spirit snapped free, and he sank down into an ecstasy that was torturous and excruciatingly pleasurable.

"You have a beautiful body..." Anna told him while her lips tantalized his taut muscular stomach.

He managed a thought. *With all my nicks and scars and shrapnel pits?* And felt an odd exhilaration that had nothing at all to do with where her hands and tongue were now.

"Even with all your scars...it's beautiful," she continued as her fingers traced the outline of an old injury.

The sensations he was experiencing all seemed to barricade themselves in his throbbing erection. One more touch from Anna and he knew he'd explode. He put his hands in her hair, tugging at its thick rich strands to bring her to his chest. "Anna..." he choked, crushing her to him. She lay atop him, chest to breast, belly to belly, soft thigh to his hard, leg to leg, and he began to turn, carrying her with him.

Anna braced her knee against his thigh, stopping the motion.

"If...if I could just stay up here?" she whispered.

"But I want—"

"I know...." Those were the last recognizable words between them as Anna moved her hips astride him entrancingly, so that his throbbing was meeting a soft warm welcome at the juncture of her thighs. All other sounds were the transparent delighted gasps and breaths of excited unguarded murmurings of a loving union. Her body joined his in trembling with anticipation, joined his in a rhythm as ancient as time itself, and when provocation had reached its limit, Anna collapsed upon his heaving chest, knowing that were it not for skin surrounding them, her bones would be scattering with the indescribable explosion.

Later, as their passions tamed and their ragged breathing evened out, they talked. Careful talk, so as not to mar the magic they felt, words that touched only on their dreams.... She wanted to own a bookstore, but knew nothing of business, only books. He wanted to learn to fly, but just climbing a two-foot ladder gave him chills. They spoke not a word of the unsafe past or the immediate future, which was too unpredictable.

When their voices and thoughts became faint, they slept, her hand tucked securely into his.

Anna woke to find Caburn rummaging through his clothes for a cigarette. "Have you given up your pipe?" she asked sleepily.

He looked at her, smiling. His blond hair was a mad tangle over his head and there was a mischievous glint in his eye. "Somehow a pipe doesn't taste as good after sex." He rummaged a bit more, found his cigarettes and more.

Anna returned his smile, noted the sun was trying its level best to creep through the limbs of the tall pines outside his window, and buried her head in the pillow. "I can't believe I want to, but I feel like sleeping Christmas away." His walk was springy as he came back to bed, his grin curious, so that Anna raised herself up on her elbow. "Do you know something I don't?"

He thrust out his hand. It held a small package wrapped in gold foil. "For you. Merry Christmas."

She accepted it with reluctance, with a sense of mortification. "I didn't think...I mean I did, but I didn't buy you a gift...." Tears lurked behind her eyes.

He gathered her into his arms, holding her head tight against his chest, his lips touching her hair. "Anna...Anna...you gave me my gift last night... this morning...no woman has ever touched me as you have. That's something I'll treasure for the rest of my life; a memory that will never wear out." He loosened his arms and peeled her fingers from the small package, opening it, withdrawing the gold bracelet.

"It's beautiful," Anna gasped as he fixed the clasp around her wrist.

"Not nearly as beautiful as you." He gave her a gentle kiss. "You taste sweet in the mornings." His kiss became more demanding, opening her mouth with his tongue. Anna pulled away, breathless. She lifted her eyes and met Caburn's gaze of magnetic intensity. She consented with her eyes. Her gift that so pleased him was easily given.

SHE SPENT CHRISTMAS DAY puttering around his house, wearing one of his shirts with the sleeves rolled up. They ate eggs and pancakes for Christmas dinner, drank copious amounts of coffee and hot chocolate, and eyed one another, sometimes cautiously, sometimes openly. They feasted on one another's body, Anna delivering herself into hands that reached for her, filled with a craving to seize every part of him. She felt wanton, lascivious, happy.

She stayed with him. Each time she suggested going home, he pressed himself against her, running his tongue up her neck to her ear, masterfully unbuttoning the shirt that draped her, until she stood before him naked, her heart accelerating. Then the part of him she had come to know so well would burgeon, and she couldn't leave him like *that*.

Anna was amazed that the hours they spent together, the hours of growing familiarity, did not
lessen their need for each other. It became sharper,
more defined, more intense, if that was possible. On
the last day of the holiday a new element found its
way into their lovemaking, a kind of desperation fed
by the knowledge that what they shared was coming
to an end. And it did have to end. She knew it now;
that was why they couldn't speak of the future.
There couldn't be a future between them. His prin-
ciples and her pregnancy forbade it.

She had been reminded of being pregnant only
once... when Caburn's hands were grasping her
hips he had innocently noted she was fleshing out
finally. Her thinness had worried him.

They put off leave-taking until the last moment.
She was dressed fully for the first time in days, suffering a letdown feeling. She didn't want to go home
to her own house, her lonely old house. She sat
across from Caburn at the marble-topped table, sipping on coffee. She had taken the tree down, packed
the decorations into paper bags to transport home.
"I can say in all honesty that I've never had a holiday quite like this one." Her voice was tremulous.

"Me neither." Caburn was selecting a certain
thought, at random he was sure. His brain wouldn't
betray him like that. Not yet, not when he knew the
time wasn't right. That it was still too soon—sexual
chemistry aside. It must be the *old* brain, he thought.
The one hidden behind layers of bark, a primordial
instinct having to do with the preservation of the
human species. Yet the thought clung like a leech
and made its treacherous way down to his tongue.
Anna was smiling when he said, "I think we ought
to get married, don't you?"

Her smile stayed frozen in place because she had

forgotten about it. She gripped the cup, praying that she hadn't heard right, praying that this was some trick of her mind...wishful thinking gone haywire. Or maybe it was her pregnancy sending a subconscious anxious message, wild hormonal signals that affected her hearing. She was taking too long to answer because the questioning look on Caburn's face was dissolving. "Did you say...?"

"Let's get married."

"I thought I was hallucinating. Too much coffee, or sex." Her attempt at humor went flat. A lump grew in her throat. She tried to swallow it again and again.

A kind of coldness came into Caburn's brain as he watched her. He wanted to touch her hand, take her into his arms, bury his face in her lovely scented hollows, and...yes!...beg. Her large dark eyes met his. They looked enormous, pupils and iris equally dark and merging pools of...that mystery he couldn't define or find answer to.

Anna saw his face changing, going all lined and haggard, his lids beginning to shutter his eyes slowly as if drawing a shade.

"I can't marry you." It was an almost inaudible whisper.

"Anna. I've never asked anyone to marry me. I thought to once, but you know about that, and I've been singularly grateful that I didn't. Now I feel singularly damned. It can't be that you're still mourning Nesmith...."

"I'm not."

"We've shared more than sex, more than our bodies these past four days. I know it. You know it. Are you saying you don't love me?" He held his breath. He was putting it on the line.

"That's not a fair question." Her voice was somewhat louder, but trimmed with conflicting emotion. She took a sip of the coffee, a tiny bit of activity just so she didn't have to look at him, just so he couldn't see her face, her mouth. She felt leaden and numb. "How I feel about you doesn't matter now. I can't marry you."

An investigator, he was trained to catch every nuance in voice, every telling sound of emphasis on a syllable or word. An emphasis that was often the turning point in a case, often the only warning of danger or a nagging premonition. "*Now?*" he thrust at her. "Why not *now*? What's happened that you haven't told me?"

"Nothing." *Except that I'm having a baby.* For one horrible instant she thought she had spoken aloud. But he was still peering at her questioningly. She couldn't tell him it *might* be his baby, because *might* wasn't good enough for him. He had made that clear with Cassie. And a baby sired by Kevin would always be there between them, a reminder. Because, no matter what, her baby was going to know its heritage, good or bad. It was her child's right and she wouldn't be selfish enough to take that away from him...her. Oh, it was going to be so hard. At times she couldn't even recall the sound of Kevin's voice. She didn't want to remember it, but she had to, just in case. "Caburn, please...please don't ask me to explain. It's not something I can tell you."

He wanted to grab her, shake some sense into her, make her trust him beyond all reason. "You can tell me anything, Anna. *Anything*. It won't make any difference to me. You went to the doctor for a checkup. Are...are you sick?" There was terror and dread in his voice. "I mean really sick. All that retching you've done. Do you have some terrible disease?"

She dropped her head into the palms of her hands, edging up to a burst of soft hysterical laughter. "No. I'm as healthy as a horse and then some."

"Then it can only be one thing," he aired bitterly. "I'm just for rebound, just someone to take up the slack, good for laughs."

She lifted her face from her hands, her delicate features set, making her voice calm. "You've never made me laugh."

"Only because you have such a primitive sense of humor."

He was pulling himself away from rejection. Oh, how she could recognize those signs. She could see it in the way he moved his hands, the way he flexed his shoulders, the way he inhaled and exhaled slowly. That she was hurting him left an unbearable ache deep inside her. "I don't want to trade insults with you. I've never felt about a man the way I feel about you. It only makes things worse. It doesn't change things."

"I ask you to marry me and you offer me a puzzle. Do you think for one minute that I won't get to the bottom of this? That I won't discover what it is you're hiding?"

She blocked the urge to tell him that he would know answers soon enough, that in a few weeks time, perhaps less, considering how fast her waist was spreading, the answer would be obvious. Her shoulders drooped dejectedly. There was no good reason to prolong the implacable pain she was feeling now. "I don't think we should see one another so often anymore. I'm doing fine on my own."

A harsh sound broke from his throat. "You're not ridding yourself of me that easily."

"Take me home," she said. The words rang in her ears. How often she had said them over the past several days. And each time he had come to her, loving her, so that home was his heart, his body, his kingdom. She looked up sadly. This time he pushed away from the table, pushed away from her to locate his car keys.

14

JANUARY SWEPT in like a gray vacuum, giving Anna little cause to celebrate. State had assigned Caburn to a new case that took him to several cities, and he hadn't been in Washington for New Year's. Corruption, he told her, did not take a holiday. Her unvoiced love for him burned like a flame, scouring her soul.

New Year's Day triggered a depression that had lingered and lingered. It was like a birthday—a signpost, a milestone, a time for evaluation. The old year with all its problems, its grief and disappointments, was now officially separated from the new. Anna's private calendar was separated into *before* Caburn and *after* Caburn.

Compounding the grayness was her financial situation. She knew she had to solve problems, find solutions and keep on working. She would not, could not, afford to take a long maternity leave. Yet she didn't want to leave her baby, not in its first important year. Not ever, if she could help it. She thought longingly about owning her own bookstore. A store where she could take her baby to work with her. She began to plan, but plans with no money were useless, nothing more than airy wishfulness.

Work in Senate Research Services was never dull, yet more often than not Anna found herself daydreaming of Caburn. There he was, nuzzling her ear or the edge of her mouth, or... other places, which would set her face to burning so that she'd look up quickly to see if any of her colleagues had noticed. With a flick of an eyelash she could so realistically imagine his hands wandering over her flesh that the tips of her swelling breasts would come erect, sending delicious shafts of pleasure into her groin. She missed Caburn desperately and wished he'd wrap up the case he was working on and hurry back to Washington.

Then she began to wish he wouldn't, for she went to bed one night with her tummy only slightly rounded, and the following morning she woke up looking like a pregnant pear. And that was the day Caburn came home. She agreed to meet him at the Post Office Pavilion after work. Neutral territory and safe.

"SHOULD WE BE EATING these oysters? It's January, a month with an 'r' in it," Phipps said, but plowed the oyster onto a cracker and loaded it with horseradish, anyway.

Caburn took a swig of beer. "I'm from the plains. The only oysters I know about are mountain—"

"Never mind," Phipps rejoined quickly, popping the succulent oyster into his mouth.

"What're we doing here, anyway? Why couldn't you meet me at the office in Foggy Bottom?"

"I'm meeting Anna here. Didn't want to be late."

He caught sight of her as she took a place in the queue at the ice-cream kiosk. It was a one-sided intimacy, seeing her like this, knowing that she wasn't yet aware of him. He took in everything about her; her hair was getting longer and she had it tied back with a soft yellow ribbon; her cheeks were crimson from the cold and though he couldn't see her eyes from this distance, he knew they were wide, fringed with thick fluttering lashes. The muscles around his heart contracted. His hands itched with the need to touch her, and his lips went dry remembering the musky, sleep-scented hollows of her neck. Reluctantly he drew his gaze away, turning his attention back to Phipps. "I want to check out the Nesmith file...go over it again."

Phipps snorted. "What are you trying to do? Resurrect a dead man? The case is closed."

"There are loose ends, and I don't like loose ends. We still don't know the meaning of those codes in his calendars. I thought I could go through them and maybe get old Jake upstairs to work on them. He owes me a favor."

"Don't go strong-arming cryptanalysis," warned Phipps.

Anna had her cone now. Caburn stood up. "Would I do that?"

"Yeah, you would," his boss answered sourly. "Hey, where're you going? You leaving me to pay the check?" He got no answer. Caburn had already dissolved into the crowd....

Anna turned away from the kiosk and walked right into Caburn's arms. She saved her ice cream only in time, stretching her arm out. He hugged her against his chest, buried his face in her neck, tasting her, loving her. He slipped his arms inside her coat, drawing her hips against his. "Caburn, you idiot, you can't do that here," she hissed.

He held her, looking at her with a strange uncomposed feeling washing over him. The mystery and wariness that lodged in her eyes was still there. With the single-mindedness of a man with a purpose, he took her arm, propelling her through the crowded pavilion. "Come on, I'm taking you home."

"I have my car...."

"We'll get it later. Mine's just outside."

It was a few minutes before Anna realized he meant *his* home. Her hand fluttered to her stomach, a protective helpless gesture. "I guess you're glad to see me?" she uttered stiffly.

Dense, homeward-bound traffic held his attention, but he glanced at Anna out the corner of his eye. He was aware of a sudden rousing of his perception. There was an air of expectancy about Anna...a happening...of something to be...and it wasn't sexual. The vibes weren't right for that. She seemed fixed with some self-important feminine conceit of which he had no part, as if she no longer needed him as he needed her. He felt the urge to punish her for her infidelity—whatever it might be. "About as happy as you are to see me," he said.

"Why are you being sarcastic? I am happy to see you. I've missed you." She had to touch him. Her hand slipped along the ridge of the seat to touch the back of his neck. Her fingers toyed with a blond curl. His heart sang at her touch and he felt instant chagrin.

"I'm just tired; it's been a long three weeks," he said by way of apology. "I missed you, too. Missed everything about you."

Anna withdrew her hand, unconsciously smoothing the gray wool over her abdomen where the pleats fell like fluted stone.

His house was chilly. "I'll get the heat on," Caburn said the moment they were inside. He turned to face her. Anna thought of flying into his arms. The expression on his face, one of shifting meaning, stopped her.

"You do look as though you could use a bath and a shave. Would you like me to begin supper?" she asked, the question tentative so as not to appear too eager.

Caburn smiled his wonderful boyish grin that took away all his menace. "That's the best offer I've had in weeks. Home-cooked food. I could come home to you every day, you know."

Anna knew she was flirting with fire, knew that somehow, some way, she was going to have to break this off. To continue on this way wasn't fair to him, to her, or to the baby. "I know," she said brightly, and waved him upstairs as she went into the kitchen.

She didn't remove her coat until she heard his footsteps on the treads. Then she fluffed out the pleats, loosened the ribbon around her thickening waist, and covered it with the big barbecue apron she'd worn before. Camouflage.

CABURN PUSHED his plate away and began filling his pipe. "You did wonders considering the dregs in my refrigerator."

Anna beamed at his compliment. "There were more than dregs, and it helps to have that microwave. I wish I owned one."

He shifted in his chair. "You can own that one."

Her throat tightened, knowing full well his meaning. "No, I can't. I told you."

She had to get out from under his piercing scrutiny. For the first time she felt ill at ease in her own body, her pregnant body, which was growing by leaps and bounds. She thought he could see the way her breasts were swelling, the growing mound of her stomach. She picked up their plates and carried them into the kitchen, staying there as long as she dared. By the time she reemerged into the living room he had turned down the lights, put a record on the stereo and was lounging on one of his oversized sofas. She wandered around the room, knowing his gaze was following her. She felt molten. Molten and weak from hunger for him.

Finally she stood before the windows, looking out. It was dark and a slice of moon cast a white light on scattered puddles in the street. Then she wasn't seeing the moonlit puddles, but Caburn's reflection on the panes.

She saw him knock the ashes from his pipe, the small sound echoing in the room. He got up, moving silently toward her, and Anna knew before he reached her that his arms were going to surround her. She was ruled by her heart. She couldn't help it. She could feel the heat from his body as he closed the space between them. He placed his hands lightly on her shoulders, and they stood that way for a long moment, savoring the touch of one another, his eyes meeting hers in the glass; neither speaking in the sultry silence that says a mood has gone beyond words.

Then he lifted the hair from her neck and pressed his lips against her nape. They felt papery and dry until his tongue flicked out, tasting her, his teeth nibbling at her flesh so that wonderful chills darted throughout Anna.

"I've missed you...missed you...missed you..." Caburn muttered in a voice so guttural Anna wasn't certain of his words.

He turned her slowly in his arms, as if to prove to himself that she was truly there. The clean fragrance of soap and after-shave filled Anna's nostrils, an aphrodisiac that only tantalized the aching within her. The length of their bodies touched: knees, breasts, thighs. Anna laid her head on his shoulder while her arms crept inside his robe, circling him, holding him close. She knew where all this was leading, and because she wanted him so badly, her conscience would not let her give in so easily.

"Shouldn't I do the dishes now?"

"Later...." His lips were on her brow, her eyelids, the tip of her nose.

"We shouldn't be doing this...." Her pulse was running wild in her throat.

"Who said...?" He sounded miles away.

Anna was no longer able to preserve an air of convention. "I can't think who," she whispered as his lips claimed hers in a long drugging kiss that left them breathless and aroused, lost for thoughts and words. His tongue was an entity having a life of its own, thrusting into her again and again until Anna was filled with the exquisite agony of want.

He moved his lips a fraction from hers. "Are we going to make love right here in front of the window?"

Anna found that she could not speak. She shook her head, and he took her hand as they went from lamp to lamp, switching them off. She told herself this was folly. Suppose he noticed that her waist had thickened...that her breasts were fuller. He pulled her over to the sofa. In a moment they were naked. His hands softly brushed her body as if to imprint it forever in his memory. And he did notice. Her heart stopped.

"You're tactless," she said, her voice quavering.

He laughed throatily. "Did I say I didn't like it?"

"You're thinking—"

"This is what I'm thinking...." He gently touched her nipples with his fingers, and his mouth descended warm and moist. His lips curled around them so that pleasure shot through her until she was bereft of air because she forgot to breathe. She felt him surge out, uncoiling and swelling against her thigh. His fingertips trailed up the inside of her legs, featherlike patterns she tried to keep in her mind and could not. Her hand went to him, moving over him. The pitch of desire was intolerable. She did not feel the rough fabric of the sofa beneath her, only

Caburn and the fiery path of his tongue and the burning touch of his fingers.

Of their own accord, her legs spread, beckoning him, commanding his hot flesh, unable to bear the delay. She kissed his chest, his nipples, treating them to moist little forays until he groaned and lost all restraint and thrust into her. The end came quickly, yet they clung to one another, prolonging the sensations.

Long minutes passed before he spoke. "Sleepy?"

She smiled against the thick cords of his neck where the vein still pounded. She didn't want to spoil her sense of satiety by talking or moving. She just wanted to lie there and wallow in it. "Drained. I need to shower though, and get dressed."

He shifted his weight off her and sat up, leaving her free as his hand went out to the lamp.

"No!" she said sharply, and in the dark scouted for her dress, found his robe instead and wrapped that around her.

"What's this? It's a little late to be going all shy on me. I know every inch of your body. Why hide it?"

She was thinking that there were far more inches now than the last time they made love. "It's still chilly in here is all."

"I thought we took the temperature up several hundred degrees," he said grinning.

"Just like a man to brag. I'm going to bathe." She gathered up her clothes and made for the stairs.

ANNA STOOD at the top of the stairs, wrapped once again in his robe, her hair shower damp with tendrils clinging to her slender neck. "What happened to my clothes? I left them lying on your bed."

Caburn came out of the kitchen, a teapot in his hand, and stood at the bottom of the steps looking up. He had donned a caftan, loose and flowing, that made him seem an integral part of his Mediterranean furnishings. "You're not going home."

Anna's hand fluttered to her throat. "Yes...I have to work tomorrow." A stab of panic shot through her, cold, hard, unrelenting. "Where are my clothes?"

"I've put them away. Come downstairs; we can talk."

Her hand trailed the banister. It felt cold, so cold. The expression on Caburn's face was not that of her lover. It was metamorphosing, taking on that predatory look she had seen at first meeting. Her mouth went dry. "Talk about what?" she asked almost inaudibly as she sailed past him to the marble-topped table set for tea. *He knows,* she thought. *Oh, he knows, and all is lost.*

Caburn poured tea, placing a cup before Anna. She didn't dare pick it up for fear that her trembling hands would betray her nervousness.

"All right," Caburn said, sliding into the chair opposite her and leaning forward on his elbows. "Let's hear it. What are you holding back? What are you hiding?"

Eyes cast down, Anna tightened the rope belt around her waist. "I don't know what you're talking about."

"Anna, my sweet darling Anna, I'm very good at this. I've been catching these vibes from you since Christmas, odd undercurrents—"

"You can't keep me here against my will, in... in...." She flailed her arm. "In your house...your kingdom. You can't!"

A muscle in his jaw worked; a vein throbbed in his temple. His voice went very low, yet every word was sharp. "My kingdom? I want you to share it with me, such as it is. Tell me you don't love me, tell me you never want to see me again, and I'll get your clothes and call a cab to take you home."

"You're not being fair."

She hadn't denied him. Caburn's heart thundered. He leaned back in his chair and began to pack his pipe. "I have every intention of keeping you here until I have the truth out of you."

Anna's voice and face went a little tight. "I told you before, I don't think it has anything to do with you."

"You don't think?" he repeated silkily. "What the hell are you keeping from me? What is it that you think is so terrible?"

"You're jumping to conclusions. I never said it was anything bad. You can't just keep me prisoner here. Get dressed and take me home."

He ignored her.

"I'll wear this robe home. I'll call a cab."

His arm slipped to the floor and lifted slightly to display the telephone, unplugged, with the cord trailing.

"I hid the one upstairs. Now why don't you stop being evasive like a good girl?"

"Don't patronize me! I'm so tired of being patronized by you, by Phipps...." She knew she was being unreasonable. Desperation clogged her throat. She stared at Caburn unsteadily. Her head began to reel. "Excuse me. I think I'm going to be ill."

She wasn't, but her fingers clutched the sink until she was certain her legs would hold her. She had to tell him. Her life would be in pieces again, flotsam. But Caburn had loved her for herself, made her whole again. She could spend the rest of her life on that—couldn't she? *Couldn't she?*

She washed her face, ran her fingers through her hair, presenting herself to him poised on uncertainty. He was pacing the long length of the dining and living rooms, and stopped when he heard her bare feet padding across the dhurrie rug. His expression was sober, but his eyes suddenly kindled as if he sensed her decision.

"Feel better?" he said kindly.

"I feel brutal." Her fingers rose to touch her temple, feeling it throbbing. She took a deep breath, loosening words as she exhaled. "The long and short of it is... I'm going to have a baby."

He stood rooted to the floor. He couldn't speak, but his Adam's apple betrayed him cruelly, bobbing as he tried to swallow to moisten his throat.

Anna couldn't continue to watch him. She picked a spot on the wall and talked to it. "You see, I stopped using birth control in August, and then I wasn't regular...." Her face flamed, but she was driven now to have it all said. "Kevin and I...the last time was a couple of days after my birthday. And then my world fell apart. You and I...that was three or four weeks later. Dr. Oldham can't pinpoint my delivery date. I don't know which of you is the father of my baby." Her eyes slid from the spot on the wall to Caburn. There was a wretched look of torment on his face. "May I go home now?"

"I might be the father!" he exploded gutturally. "It seems to me I've heard that one before." He didn't want to admit how that hurt, how it squeezed his soul, yet a vital thing surged up, entered his mind and stayed there.

All the color drained from Anna's face. She was drowning in the heavy depth of a dark pool. She managed somehow to float to the sofa, an unconscious regalness in her bearing as she sat on an arm. "I know you have. It's one of the reasons I didn't accept your proposal." She was going to collapse at any minute.

Caburn stalked to the window, staring out. The window where she had watched his reflection only an hour or two ago. A lifetime ago. He turned to face her, his eyes shuttered. She knew that look. Oh, she wanted this to be next week, next year, she wanted to be 109 years old, feebleminded, so that this moment would be behind her, forever in the dim past, forgotten.

He stalked the room, a caged animal looking for the way out. Finally he stopped, standing before Anna, powerful, controlled. "We'll get married this week."

She heard him, but fixed her mind on the future, on the baby that was growing inside her, on the protective wall she resolved to build around her. "It wouldn't work. You'd always be wondering...I want my baby to be loved. It has enough strikes against it as it is. And you didn't say that to Cassie twelve years ago. So why are you talking marriage to me now?"

He reeled as though struck. "I never loved Cassie. She seduced me as much as I did her." His mouth hardened into a comprehending line. "Anna, you know and I know Cassie slept her way across Kansas that summer. My brother Wally thinks Tip is his son—he loves him and adores Cassie. As far as I'm concerned that's dead wood."

"What about questionable liaisons? What about that heritage of yours, the one you want for your son?"

He shook his head, and there was a trace of a bitter smile on his lips. "Let me tell you, right now that doesn't seem important."

"What does? Chivalry? I won't marry you. Four or five months from now you might regret it. I...I couldn't take that. I want this baby. I'll be mother *and* father to it, if I have to."

He began to pace again, stopping at the table to remove a cigarette from a leather box. "Does Clara Alice know about the baby?" he asked with deceptive softness.

Anna froze. "No...and she won't." The thought of Clara Alice hovering around her, around her baby, filled Anna with rage and disgust.

He had found his leverage. It was painful, feeling like he had broken every bone in his body. "There's a price you'll have to pay for my silence."

"What price?"

"Become Mrs. Caburn."

"You just want to persecute me—"

"I want to marry you. You see, I know you want me, too, and we'll just have to make that do for starters."

"What I want is a decent home for my baby."

Caburn knew Anna's pride was talking. He struck a match and put fire to his cigarette, glaring at her through a cloud of gray smoke. "That's settled then."

Anna was hungry for stability, for shelter, for trust. She was hungry for Caburn's strength, his vulnerability, too, now that she had glimpsed it. Her answer was as ambiguous as possible without actually saying yes. "You'll have to quit smoking...it isn't good for the baby."

15

Anna finished making the bed and moved over to the window looking out onto a sun-drenched landscape. It was the last day in May. She had been married to Caburn for four months and she was 216 days pregnant—if she counted from the last Sunday in October and her first intimacy with Caburn. She always counted from that day. It wasn't provident to tempt fate. She turned away from the window as her husband stepped from the bathroom.

"Hey," he said, "you made up the bed already."

"Shouldn't I have?"

He crossed to her, touching her stomach tenderly with his fingers before pulling her to him. "No, you shouldn't. You see, I have this grand passion for you and I thought—"

She laughed. "You *always* have a grand passion. And if I indulge you this morning you'll be late for work, and if you're late for work you'll be late coming home and we have guests for dinner tonight."

He pretended a frown. "Again?"

"Is it my fault that you freeloaded off Sophia and Nancy these past twelve years?"

"I had to go somewhere to get home-cooked meals."

"Yes, well, now they expect to be reciprocated. I have to meet the realtor over at my house this morning, and I promised Lila I'd stop in for coffee and a chat."

"You're sure I can't talk you into—"

Anna laughed. "I'm positive. Now, get dressed. Breakfast will be ready in ten minutes." She began to shift away from him. He caught her wrist.

"Anna, you're happy, aren't you?" He inspected her face gravely. There was still that frailty about her features that haunted him at times.

"You know I am. Happier than I've ever been in my life. Never mind that you blackmailed me into marrying you, never mind that living with you with all your little foibles isn't easy." She lifted his scarred fingers to her lips. "Breakfast... ten minutes, okay?"

"Okay."

She was halfway to the hall when he stopped her again, as if he was just waiting for that space between them before he spoke again. There was a tautness to his stance, an expression of protectiveness toward her. "You know I'll love the baby, regardless...." He left the rest unsaid but his look was penetrating.

A fleeting frown crossed Anna's face as she fixed her eyes on Caburn. "I know you will. I trust you."

She did trust him, she thought later in the day as she was driving home from Lila's. Her heart swelled with a bliss she had not known possible. He was generous with his wealth, insisting that she furnish the nursery with only the best-quality furniture, toys and mobiles from F.O.A. Swartz, and every drawer was already crammed so full of clothes she'd have to have triplets to see them all worn.

Yet their first month of marriage had been trying. After all those weeks after Clara Alice had left, she had enjoyed being her own woman, enjoyed her independence and privacy. Giving it up had not mattered to her, but Caburn's protectiveness had nearly choked her.

One night they had been lying in bed watching television when a March of Dimes appeal came on.

"Did you hear that?" he had asked with alarm.

"I was dozing."

"They said one in every twelve births results in birth defects!"

"They weren't talking about me. Dr. Oldham says my baby is —"

"How does he know? Can he see it?"

"There's nothing wrong with me or my baby." Secretly she worried, but she didn't want worry to be put into words.

Caburn would not be pacified. He began to guard her like a samurai warrior. He insisted she quit work, avoid people who sneezed, had headaches or pimples. When her ankles swelled, he was certain she had a kidney disease; if her heart skipped a beat, he rushed her to Dr. Oldham; if she became short of breath, he was certain the baby was starving for oxygen. Then he read about the treachery of German measles.

The last straw had been in early March when a Girl Scout had knocked on the door. Caburn had glared at her. "Do you have the measles?"

Saucer-eyed and confused, the child had answered, "No, only cookies." Anna had made him buy a dozen boxes of chocolate mint.

It was laughable now, but it hadn't been then and it had taken her silken threats to sleep on the sofa before he had given her breathing room.

Caburn was everything a woman could ask for in a husband. Reasonably ask for, she amended now with an unconscious smile. But was she deluding herself, believing that he was accepting the baby as his own? Her hopes wavered, delighted one minute, bleak the next.

"Good Catholic that I am, I've solved the mystery of Nesmith's little black books," Jake said, accepting

Caburn's proffered hand. "Say, aren't you married to the Nesmith woman now? The first wife, I mean. Seems I heard—"

"You heard right, Jake." Caburn's grin was brittle. The old man cleared his throat. He was tall, in his fifties, with a craggy, smile-creased face, and he was uncomfortable. "Well now! Maybe I ought to just pass this information on over to Phipps. You get it from him."

"Quit stalling, Jake. What does being Catholic have to do with those calendars?"

"Listen, Caburn, if you weren't married to the woman and all, I wouldn't mind telling you, but...."

Caburn felt his guts gripping inward. "Those codes have something to do with Anna?"

"Yeah." His face going pink, Jake pushed the books toward Caburn.

"I'm not budging from this room until you tell me, Jake." Caburn's voice was suddenly menacing.

Jake cleared his throat. "Well...see those?" He tapped one of the pages. "That's the genetic sign for female. Every so often you'll find the letter *C* with an *A* inside it."

"So?"

"So, *C* stands for contact. *A* for Anna."

"Make sense." His nerves were stretched tight, the pain in his stomach getting worse.

"It's the rhythm system...birth control. Some Catholics, among other people, use it to keep from having babies. Looks like Nesmith, uh, kept track of every time he, uh, did it...with Anna."

The corners of Caburn's mouth were turning down, his eyes going incredibly hard. Jake shifted on the little stool he was sitting on. "Nesmith was one son-of-a—"

"How does it work?" Caburn shot at him.

It took Jake a few minutes to explain. "This is

rough, you understand," he ended finally. "I mean, Nesmith obviously wasn't taking her temperature, but he was as careful as he could be. It doesn't look as though they were doing it any too often, and only in her safe times...." Jake trailed off, thinking maybe he'd gotten carried away. After all, they were talking about Caburn's wife. And Caburn had a reputation for being dangerous, except that right this minute he had a funny look on his face, like maybe he couldn't breathe. Jake leaned forward. "Say, you want some water or something?"

Caburn didn't answer. He was trying to absorb Jake's words, and the impact of them slammed into his brain. "You're sure?" he said finally.

"I fed it into the computers again and again. That's all they came up with. I'm sure. Besides, Betsy and I, uh, we've been using this system for nigh on twelve years. After eight kids, we had to do something." He gave an embarrassed laugh.

"It really works?"

"If you're careful and don't go doing anything rash." Jake tapped the black books with his finger. "Nesmith here was *very* careful."

Caburn's mind was racing backward, remembering, seeing himself comforting Anna. Comforting? Loving her. The sound of her voice reverberated inside his skull. *"Do you know what he did that hurts the most? He let her have a baby. I've been trying so hard to get pregnant."*

And so she had, secretly, Anna had thought. But Nesmith had caught on that Anna had stopped her pills. She hadn't been devious enough.

Outside the laboratory and away from Jake's prying eyes, Caburn leaned against the wall, suddenly weak. Anna was pregnant with his child. The realization shouldn't make him feel so giddy. He loved the unborn baby anyway, had caught Anna's excitement, had shared the hard moments with her and the funny ones, too.

He made a decision. Anna didn't doubt his love, not for her or the child. He was certain of that. He wouldn't burden her with what he had just discovered. There was no sense in reopening old wounds. He didn't want anything to come between them now, not when she was so close to her time.

ON HER 256TH DAY of pregnancy Anna mused that it was a kind of justice engineered by God, but she knew Caburn arose every morning with a sinking sensation in his stomach and she was awakening with hers literally blossoming.

"If you could just sleep on your other side instead of pushing up against me at night, I might get some sleep," Caburn lamented as he lifted up on one elbow and kissed her burgeoning belly. "Mt. Everest kicked all night long again. How can you sleep through that?"

"I could sleep on the sofa downstairs," she answered in honeyed tones.

"Nix that. Wives sleep with their husbands." He pressed his lips to the throbbing blue vein on her brow while his hand roamed gently over her full breasts. "Nice...warm...full," he said lazily. "Wives also do other things with their husbands."

Her pulses quickened. "Full is right," she laughed. "Stop that." She pushed him away, marveling though at the sensations that bypassed her protruding stomach to settle between her thighs. She had not liked growing shapeless before Caburn's eyes, and had grown shy at letting him see her naked, but he had not minded, nor had his ardor slackened these past weeks. "We can't do it anymore."

He kissed the soft bloom on her cheek. "You're sure?"

"Positive. Dr. Oldham said it wouldn't be the proper way to introduce a baby to sex."

He moved his hands with a sense of keen disappointment and folded them behind his head. "The Sybaritic old goat."

Anna stretched languorously. "You're the Sybarite."

She got up and fluffed out the flowing gossamer caftan that served as her nightgown. The pressure on her kidneys was powerful these past few days. Today was no different and she spent a few minutes in the bathroom, but for some reason this morning she couldn't get any relief. As she made her way back to bed she did not feel the first contraction as a recognizable pain. But the second one, hard, pulsating and stabbing, left no doubt. *Oh, no. Dear God,* she prayed. *No. Ten more days, please.* A moan like that of a tiny crippled animal broke from her throat.

"Anna?"

An insidious sense of helplessness overtook her. "I think I'm going to have this baby," she rasped.

Misunderstanding, Caburn grinned. "Tell me something new."

"I mean...now. Today. I mean...." A low whimper escaped her as another contraction struck. A thin sheen of sweat began forming on her forehead.

He was thunderstruck. "You can't!"

Clarity shot through Anna. He'd been counting, too, she thought wretchedly. Oh, why couldn't she have managed another ten days...then she could have been certain. Certain of her baby's father. She was impotent against what was happening to her. She looked at Caburn, her expression desolate. "I don't see how I can help it."

A sweeping chill raced down Caburn's spine. It was happening. Now. Today. He was going to be a daddy. His mouth went so suddenly dry he could barely speak. "Anna..." he croaked. "I'd better call—" He dashed naked from the bed, speeding past Anna into the hall and down the stairs.

Despite her woe, Anna couldn't keep from smiling. He had fled right past the telephone near their bed. So much for Caburn in an emergency, she thought, then was overcome with another gripping pain that left her mindless of all else.

"Did you get in touch with Dr. Oldham?" she wanted to know when he came tearing back into the room. Caburn looked at her blankly.

"I called Phipps."

She was trying to pull on stockings and gave it up. "Phipps? But...why?"

"I—his was the only number I could remember."

Anna wanted to laugh, but feared what it might do. "I'll be dressed in a minute. Why don't you get my suitcase into the car." He hurried to do her bidding until Anna stopped him. "Don't you think you ought to put on your pants first?"

A look of stark surprise washed over him. Then he stopped in the middle of the room, dropped the suitcase and came to her, kneeling down in front of her as she sat on the bed. "Darling, are you sure? Are you all right? Does it hurt?"

"The way you're squeezing my hands does." He loosened them at once. She leaned over as best she could and kissed him. "Yes, to all three questions."

"Are you frightened?" He wanted to imbue her with his strength, his love, the fearsome happiness he was feeling this moment.

Knowing that this was a thing that no one could do for her, Anna put on a brave show of indifference. "A little. I've never had a baby before, you know." She traced his brow, the line of his jaw with her fingers. She couldn't bear it if he abandoned her now. "You're going to be there the whole time, aren't you?"

"Every minute."

IT WAS A FAST DELIVERY for which the entire maternity department of Women's Hospital was thankful, for Anna was exceedingly vocal during the last hard stages of labor. When she was finally wheeled into delivery from the labor room, Caburn slumped against the wall in the hospital corridor, drained.

"Just a few more minutes," he said to Phipps who had arrived at the hospital almost on their heels. "Thank you for coming. I don't think I could have managed by myself."

Phipps harrumphed and cleared his throat. "Glad to do it, Francis. Glad to do it." But he knew with a certainty that he would never set foot in a maternity ward again. He was as uncomfortable as a jar-trapped fly. And that's what he wanted to do right now—fly, but Caburn looked as though he needed moral support. There was a wild frightened look in his eyes, like that of a trapped animal, and he was drenched with sweat. "Bad show in there, I guess," Phipps said with sympathy.

"No...no, it went real well. Got any tobacco, Phipps? I'm fresh out."

"Sorry, I came away without my pipe. Louise practically pushed me out the door."

Caburn looked crestfallen. Phipps searched his mind for some tidbit with which to occupy Caburn, distract him from what was going on behind those doors. He had just the thing.

"Say, Francis, remember those calendars of Nesmith's? Old Jake up in cryptanalysis finally had a chance to glance at them and snapped to the mystery code right away. He says, uh, never mind," Phipps

said, catching the sudden savage gleam fused in
Caburn's gray eyes. Lord! he thought, he should
have had more sense than to offer such a bromide to
calm Caburn down at a time like this. Before Phipps
could repair his faux pas, Dr. Oldham emerged from
delivery.

"Your wife and daughter are doing fine, Mr. Caburn; the nurses will have them cleaned up in a few
minutes, if you want to ...."

Caburn was conscious of his own body with unusual intensity. He knew he was numbed, all senses
going dormant as his head tilted back and he slid
slowly down the corridor wall.

The two older men looked down at Caburn, one
with his mouth agape, the other resigned.

"He'll never live this down in the department,"
Phipps said, grinning.

Dr. Oldham sighed heavily. "I'll send a nurse to
revive him." And he moved off down the corridor
shaking his head.

UNOBSERVED, ANNA STOOD on the threshold of her
two-month-old daughter's room and watched her
husband carefully and tenderly lift a tiny blanket up
to an even tinier chin. Caburn was all that she could
ask for in a father...more, if that was possible. She
had tried to push aside the troubling question of
Katie's paternity, and most days it stayed locked in
the far recesses of her mind, but at times like these,
when Caburn was being so tender, it rose up to
haunt her.

She never sensed in him any indecision, never
sensed in him a lack of caring or love for her
daughter, and that was the problem. Even when she
had talked to Caburn's mother on the telephone, she
found herself saying carefully, "*I* named *my* baby

Kathryn," as if including Caburn was taking too much for granted, or flirting with a fragile flame of hope. She just couldn't make herself use the plural *we*.

She thought of Katie as *her* daughter, and when she did there came this warm rush of feeling that she had created another human being out of her own flesh and blood. A tie that, no matter what, could never be broken, never be undone.

She wanted Caburn to share that sense of creation, but she hadn't known how to broach the subject with him; she knew they had to talk about it and she knew what she was going to have to do.

The rustling of her caftan caught Caburn's attention. He looked over his shoulder, smiling.

"I thought all babies came bald. I can't get over Katie having such a cap of red curls."

"All those vitamins I took," Anna answered softly, feeling her heart swell with pride.

"Or chocolate chip ice cream," he teased, switching the lamp on low before he approached his wife and put his arm around her waist. He led her into their bedroom and pulled her down beside him on the bed. "Something's troubling you, Anna. I've noticed you wearing a frown when you thought I wasn't looking. Are you unhappy? Have I done something wrong?" Dr. Oldham had carefully explained about postpartum blues, cluing Caburn for symptoms.

"I'm not saying she's suffering from them," Dr. Oldham had said, "but she's a bit more moody than I like my new mothers, and considering the shocks she's had to her system in the space of a year...."

Anna was hesitating, knowing Caburn's gaze was stalking her every gesture. She searched for the right words, not finding them, but going on anyway.

"I...darling...would you like to have another baby right away?"

Caburn was incredulous. "No! Give me time to get used to Katie...diapers and 2:00 A.M. feedings.... What made you raise a question like that?"

She pressed her lips into his neck so that he couldn't see her face. "Because...because there is still the question...." Her throat tightened as she tried to say the painful words. "If only I could've waited another ten days, or even a week, to have Katie, then we'd know...for certain...." She felt him stiffen and lifted her face to his. The tenderness in his expression was gone, replaced by a dampish fury he was trying to control. Anna's heart lurched with dread and despair. She went on doggedly, whispering, "I love you for loving Katie, but I want us to have a baby together. I want...." She dropped her head into her hands. "Oh, I'm doing this so badly."

He took her hands from her face and pulled her into his lap. "No, you're not. But I didn't know you were concerned so about Katie and me."

"I can't help it."

"Don't cry...don't cry. You're tearing me apart. Stop that and listen to me. I should have told you this before, but I didn't want to open old wounds."

Anna listened, staring at Caburn in a kind of ethereal disbelief as he related what Jake had said about Kevin's calendars. She did not feel any anger now, only relief, as if a great dam of hurt had been released and left to wash away. At first she did not reply; the information about the calendars was astonishing. "He must have known the very day I stopped taking my pills," she said wonderingly.

"No doubt," Caburn replied dryly, tiring of discussing Nesmith, whom he hoped was getting his just deserts from St. Peter. "Katie is mine," he said fiercely. "I don't see how you couldn't see that." He was truly miffed now. "She looks just like me."

"Yes, she does, doesn't she?"

Anna had what she wanted...a home, a husband who loved her, a baby. She felt whole and it made her strong. She slid her arms around Caburn's neck. "You're vain, darling. I never noticed that before. Are you going to be one of those fathers who never lets his daughter out of his sight, who demands—"

His arms tightened around her. "I have a demand right now. I'm hungry...starving...."

"We just ate."

He bent his head, inhaling the fragrance of her; the scent of musk, of flowers and...baby powder. "Not for what I'm hungry for, we didn't."

"Oh? What would that be?" Passion made her lids heavy, her lips form a seductive moue, her breasts swell with desire while Caburn told her explicitly of his appetite.

"I seem to have acquired a taste for the same things..." she said, while parts of her that had lain dormant began to ignite at his touch.

"Don't let me hurt you." A rending sigh tore from his throat as his body closed over hers. "It's been so long...."

Hours later as they lay with arms and legs entwined, Anna trailed a fingertip down his hard muscular chest. "Caburn?"

He heard the smile in her voice. "What?"

"Did you really faint when Dr. Oldham told you we had a girl?"

He caught the *we* and sighed happily. Acceptance, reality and fantasy had merged into one. He had never lied to her, but a man had to draw a line somewhere. "No." Her fingertips trailed awfully close to a part of him that was easily aroused. "Well...maybe...."

"I'll love you for it, if you did."

"Show me."

"You mean like this...and this...?"

A keening sound of pleasure escaped him. "Yes. Exactly...."

Exclusive Harlequin home subscriber benefits!
- SPECIAL LOW PRICES for home subscribers only
- CONVENIENCE of home delivery
- NO CHARGE for postage and handling
- FREE *Harlequin Romance Digest*®
- FREE BONUS books
- NEW TITLES 2 months ahead of retail
- MEMBER of the largest romance fiction book club in the world